## He could almost taste her.

Damien's breath caught. His chest constricted and his palms dampened.

*Look at the fire burning in her eyes, the soft ruby dewiness of her lips—a peach ripe for the picking. Take a bite, Damien.*

He licked his lips and felt his fangs descend.

"Mr. Hancock? Are you all right?" A soft voice broke through the cloud in his mind, interrupting his delicious thoughts.

"Emma McGovern?" he choked. He had to get ahold of himself. He took another deep breath. Nonsense. He was Damien Hancock. Adept. Master of the Occult. He'd trained for many years, honing his focus, his control.

He would not fall victim to a foolish gypsy girl's curse.

## CYNTHIA COOKE

Ten years ago, Cynthia Cooke lived a quiet, idyllic life caring for her beautiful eighteen-month-old daughter. Then peace gave way to chaos with the birth of her boy/girl twins. Hip-deep in diapers and baby food and living in a world of sleep deprivation, she kept her sanity by reading romance novels and dreaming of someday writing one. She counts her blessings every day as she fulfills her dreams with the love and support of good friends, her very own hunky hero and three boisterous children, who constantly keep her laughing and her world spinning. Cynthia loves to hear from her readers. Visit her online at http://www.cynthiacooke.com.

# RISING DARKNESS

## CYNTHIA COOKE

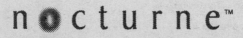

Silhouette Books

nocturne™

SILHOUETTE BOOKS

ISBN-13: 978-0-373-61770-8
ISBN-10:    0-373-61770-4

RISING DARKNESS

www.silhouettenocturne.com

Printed in U.S.A.

Dear Reader,

I love dark and stormy nights, fog-shrouded paths, getting lost in creepy, meandering mazes and exploring crumbling gothic castles. I cut my teeth on old Vincent Price movies and black-and-white vampire classics. These were the images roaming through my mind while I was setting the scenes for *Rising Darkness*.

Grab a steaming cup of Earl Grey, kick up your feet and take a journey into rural England, where all those wonderful epics of the past were created! In our world of DARK ENCHANTMENTS, dreams aren't always what they seem, wolves aren't always beasts and men, no matter how hot and sexy they appear, aren't always human.

So, don't be surprised if you find yourself falling in love with a vampire. I did! In the magical world of DARK ENCHANTMENTS anything can, and usually will, happen.

Enjoy!

Cynthia Cooke

Come visit me at www.cynthiacooke.com.

Visit all the nocturne authors at www.nocturneauthors.com.

How lucky am I that I was able to write a series with the ladies who helped make me the writer I am today. I could never express how much they all mean to me! They are more than just great friends, they are my sisters. To Nina Bruhns, Michele Hauf, and Pat White: writing this series has been a fantastic journey I could not have made without you. And to Gail Ranstrom, who has pulled me out of the fire more than once. I would never want to face the challenge of writing without any of you! I love you all!

Four hundred years ago a secret, hermetic order was created by the first Earl of St. Yve and a handful of initiates who pledged their lives to keep the world safe from evil paranormal beings. Ever since, the Cadre has been dedicated to maintaining the delicate balance between the mortal and Dark realms through research and observation of otherworldly entities. Seldom does the Cadre interfere.

But not all mortals seek peaceful understanding between the realms. In recent decades, an opposing force has been created by the British Security Service. This covert group, called P-Cell, has but one directive: destroy paranormal creatures of all kinds.

As the two organizations fight faithfully for their separate causes, unbeknownst to either of them the dark forces of evil gather, preparing to overtake the mortal realm....

# Prologue

*England, 1761*

On the night of the Equinox, a devil's moon pierced the treetops, casting silver light into the clearing. Camilla lay back on the luxurious fur by the roaring fire and watched storm clouds race by. She heard the solemn rattle and jingle of the caravan making its way down the hill and into the valley, knowing her family's *vardo* would be among them. Knowing she would never see them again.

She sighed deeply, then smiled as her new husband knelt beside her, his sunkissed hair shimmering in the flame's light. "Are you ready, my sweet?"

She knew how lucky she was, knew English gentle-
men did not marry poor gypsy girls, but that's exactly
what he'd done. He'd walked into their camp, even as
her people were loading their wagons, and begged her
to stay with him. Demeter the Gypsy King married them
on the spot as her mamma wept tears of joy, knowing
she'd be protected now, and living in privilege and
wealth.

A mischievous grin lifted William's lips. He pushed
up her blouse, ripping the gossamer fabric. The fire's
heat warmed her as he caressed her breasts, softly at
first, then harder, using the palm of his hand, the tips
of his fingers, the dull edge of his nails. His fingers
kneaded and pinched the sensitive nubs, until she ached
to push herself closer, wanting more of his sweet touch.

"Do you love me?" she asked, and swallowed a
nervous giggle even as the warmth spreading through
her veins clouded most coherent thought except the
longing, the wanting, the fire surging within her.

"I love every inch of you." His tongue swept inside her
mouth, tasting, devouring. She pulled him closer, wanting
his chest to push into her breasts, wanting the feel of him,
his touch, his taste, his scent to cover her—everywhere.

Her breath quickened as his lips moved over hers,
hard and demanding. Then he moved lower, suckling
her breast, sending a spike of pleasure zipping straight
to the core between her legs. She loved how much he
wanted her.

Somewhere in the deep recesses of her mind, she
heard the silent approach of her wolves. One by one,

they encircled the clearing, sitting between the rose quartz pieces she'd placed at the five points surrounding the fire. Their opalescent eyes caught the flame's reflection and shone red in the night. She smiled, then gasped as William's hand reached beneath her long colorful skirt and raked up her thighs.

He stroked her moist intimate parts softly, with one finger, then two. He pushed inside her. She drew a quick breath, her eyes widening as his fingers moved in and out of her in quick succession. Liquid warmth melted her insides, heating her to a frenzy, and she could no longer think how awkward it was, all she could do was feel how much she wanted him.

She squirmed, trying to draw him deeper. He shifted, moving on top of her, his heaviness covering her, his hard sex touching her soft curls, pushing, probing. This was where he belonged, where she'd wanted him to be since the first moment she'd been lost in the depths of his forest-green eyes, since the moment his raw masculine voice had scraped across her senses.

His thumb moved over the small nub between her folds. "Please," she begged, afraid he would stop, but not sure what was happening, and slightly afraid her lungs would burst with her next breath.

Without warning, he thrust into her. White-hot pain pierced her belly. She cried out, biting down on her lower lip. He halted, waiting.

"Hush, the worst is over. Now you will stretch, wrapping around me as though we are two parts of one, meant to be together."

She felt him melding into her skin and knew he was right. They were meant to be together.

Forever.

He started to move. Slowly at first, pulling himself out of her. Little by little, she felt his hard warmth withdrawing and she almost cried with the loss. "No," she murmured. He pushed forward until the length of him filled her insides. She expanded around him, tight like a satin glove.

"Oh, darling, we fit together so nicely, as if we were made for this moment, made to be together."

"Two pieces of a whole," she whispered and lost the thought as he pulled out of her once more, then slid back in.

"Do not do it again," she begged, trying to clamp her legs around him, but the harder she squeezed, the closer to an unknown brink it sent her. She was losing control of herself in sensations she'd never felt before, and it thrilled and scared her at the same time. She was approaching a cliff, and feared what would happen if she fell.

"Do what?" he said with a laugh as the fire's flames danced in his eyes.

"Do not leave me," she begged, holding him tighter, as his quickened movements pushed her closer and closer to that unknown edge where the heavens weep and the eagles cry with the absolute joy of being alive.

He shifted her body, pulling her forward, and rocked, bucking his hips until the fire swept up and consumed her, hurling her over the edge. She screamed and the wolves tilted back their heads and howled, paying homage to the bloodred moon.

She could think no more, nor move, could only breathe, and feel him, the man she loved with all her heart, wrapped around her.

A horse snorted and stamped its foot as it entered the clearing. The wolves stood, growling. Camilla pulled herself out of her stupor and opened her eyes. William looked up, his face frozen, his jaw hard.

Fear tensed Camilla's heart. "William?" she whispered, her voice breaking.

A flaxen-haired woman in soft velvet sat proudly on a snow-white stallion, her icy-blue gaze narrowing with cold hatred. "What do we have here?"

William stood, righting his clothes and leaving Camilla cold and alone to fend for herself. Quickly, she stood behind him, pulling the animal skin up to cover herself from the lecherous stares of the four men flanking the woman's sides.

"When we are married, William, I won't cater to you rutting with gypsy whores."

"Amelia," William cajoled, muttering platitudes, but Camilla didn't hear them. She couldn't. Her mind was screaming. What did she mean, *when we are married?* William was *her* husband. Maybe not in the eyes of England, not yet, but that was just a formality. He'd said so himself. Hadn't he?

"William?" she said tentatively.

He turned and looked at her, but the man standing before her now wasn't the man who'd just made love to her, this man was a stranger. There was no warmth, no sparkle of love in his eyes. Instead, they glinted with triumph, with laughter. The corner of his mouth lifted in a smirk, "Sorry, sweets, but you really should have known." He walked toward the woman with the long blond tresses and touched her golden hair. "I'd do anything to make you happy, Amelia. You know that."

She nodded at him. "Then tell the girl to go away and to never show her dirty face to me again."

"You won't have to look on her again. I promise." Long slender fingers that had just taken Camilla to places she'd never been before, moved up the woman's thigh, stroking her beneath the soft blue velvet of her riding gown.

"No," Camilla whimpered as raw pain burst within her. Tears flooded her eyes. He'd deceived her, deceived them all and now she was left here alone. She dropped to her knees, her hands reaching toward the sky, her head tipped back as a roar of heartbreak erupted from her chest to fill the night.

The wolves howled with her, a cacophony of torment.

"Call off your beasts," William snapped. "And stop that wailing!"

But she couldn't stop, any more than she could stop the thunder from assaulting the sky.

"I said stop!" He stormed toward her and struck her hard across the face.

She gasped, standing, then stared at him in frozen shock, her hand rubbing the sting from her cheek. "You said you loved me."

His gaze hardened. "How could you expect me to love a gypsy nothing like you? I only wanted to part those lovely virgin thighs." He leaned in close. "And you were well worth the wait, darling. Worth the game. Maybe later, we can play it again, eh?" He grabbed her bottom, and gave it a hard squeeze.

"You will never be happy with her," Camilla gritted. "You will never know love. Your soul will never know peace as it will be forever searching for me, for my love."

"You?" he started to laugh. Not just a chuckle, but a full-throated laugh that started deep in his belly and bubbled forth like sour frothy milk.

Cold fury unlike anything she'd ever felt before filled her. She stood, lifting her hands toward the sky, dropping the fur and turning in a tight circle.

> *"Circle marked upon the ground;*
> *"Wolves moving round*
> *"Incense rising to the sky*
> *"My power now is moving high*
> *"Chant the words and ring the bell;*
> *"Work the magick, weave the spell.*
> *"Forever you will search for love that can never be found*
> *"Not even after your corpse lies cold in the ground."*

"Witch, witch!" Amelia screamed. "Stop her."

Camilla turned faster. William groped, trying to stop her.

*"Golden beauty you will bear."*

He grasped her hair.

*"A lineage of pain to befall your heirs."*

He yanked hard, stopping her, holding her fast with her back pressed up against his chest.

*"Tragedy will be your legacy."*

Her eyes pinned the woman, her red-hot gaze melting Amelia's icy-blue stare and turning it to a puddle of fear. Camilla smiled. *"Your children's children will never know love, for the moment they do, my curse will rain down from above."*

"Kill her," Amelia screamed.

Consumed with pain and hatred, Camilla barely felt herself being lifted into William's arms—

*"Asmos,"* she yelled. "Hear my plea. Take my heart, my soul. Give my vengeance life."

—barely heard William mutter, "Die, witch," as he dropped her.

—barely felt the flames bite, as the demon's essence poured into her, every orifice expanded, filling with liquid heat that cooled, becoming sluggish and thick. She couldn't breathe. Muscle spasms cramped her stomach. Laughter reverberated through her mind, and she knew she wasn't alone.

She'd called Asmos, the demon of wrath. *And he'd come.*

She stood in the middle of the fire, and yet, the flames parted, dancing and licking her feet, but not touching her. Searing tendrils of pain grasped her insides. Fear slammed into her chest, as she bent over and clutched herself. Blood flowed from her nose and between her legs. She vomited, expelling all that was human as demon strength and power filled her, possessing her.

The wolves cried in disharmony their pain and anguish. For her?

She looked at them, looked into their eyes and reached deep into their minds. *Don't be afraid, my pets. Our time has come. Our night of vengeance has just begun.* They stood as one, howling a song of unity of spirit. Camilla straightened, standing proud, her lips curving into a dangerous smile.

Amelia screamed, turned her stallion and rode quickly into the night. Her four escorts didn't follow, but instead stared mesmerized by Camilla's beauty, by the fire alive in her eyes.

"How?" William asked, backing away from her.

She could feel Asmos's strength pulsing through her, giving her vitality and a yearning she'd never felt before. The horses neighed, their eyes wide with fear as she drew closer.

They pulled back, their hooves lifting and falling in a nervous dance.

"Shh," she whispered, calming the one closest to her, her sharp ruby-red nail lightly stroking down the long column of its neck, breaking open the skin. Blood ran in small rivulets, its coppery scent sending the wolves into a frenzy of hunger.

In sheer terror, the horse bolted upright, knocking its rider to the ground. He ran screaming into the forest.

Chaos ensued. Horses raced in every direction, men screamed, wolves attacked, making a merry chase.

And then there was William.

His eyes were wide. He no longer looked at her naked body with lust; no longer did she hear his laughter at her pain and humiliation. Now, all she saw on his face was fear, and she liked it.

As before, she wanted more.

She wanted to hear him scream.

She lunged.

# Chapter 1

*Present Day, England*

Desperation bordering on the edge of insanity filled Emma McGovern as the wolves' howling broke through the stillness of the early evening. She stood at the window, looking out onto the bleak countryside, the raucous baying bringing a tremble to her fingers and a burning sensation to the scars along her cheek. Phantom pains, she'd been told, but that didn't make them hurt less, or make the memories any less vivid.

"They're back, Lucia," Emma said without turning to look at the woman who was bending into the oven and basting the roast. The rich aroma of tender pork and glazed vegetables wafted through the kitchen but couldn't warm the chill in Emma's bones, nor mask the underlying scent of fear.

Lucia closed the oven with a sharp thud, then turned and opened a cabinet next to the stove and pulled out an antique tin. She removed the lid and took out a brooch fashioned with dried heather and gardenias. "Here, put this on," she said.

"It's beautiful," Emma murmured, then lifted the brooch to her nose and breathed deeply. Instantly, she pulled away, her face twisting in revulsion. "Eww. What is it?"

"Fish oil. It will protect you from the beasts. Now put it on and wear it, at least until the night of the Equinox has passed," Lucia insisted, and returned the tin to the cabinet.

Reluctantly, Emma pinned the brooch to her lace-trimmed top, knowing deep down that nothing would protect her from the beasts. Her destiny was catching up with her. "It will never end, will it, Lucia? Every year I think, this year will be different, but then the wolves come back." She stepped over to the window, watching, waiting for the inevitable.

Lucia shook her head. "I will find a way to break the curse. Gypsy magic created it, gypsy magic can destroy it. In the meantime, you must take precautions."

"I know." Emma gave her a half-hearted smile. "You don't have to worry on that front. Love isn't in the cards for me." Emma took a sip from her tea, and quickly averted her gaze. She didn't need a curse to keep love from her doorstep. Even if she could find love out here in the middle of nowhere, love would take one look at the scars on her face, turn and run.

Lucia's voice softened. "You can still have companionship, Emma. Friendship and a deep mutual caring are very important in any relationship. But you'll never find even that if you don't ever leave the house. Take a chance. Venture into the village. Meet people."

"So I can have what Mum and Dad had?"

"Exactly."

How could Emma explain that she wanted more than a half-hearted relationship based on mutual interests? She wanted...she blew out a sigh. She wanted what she couldn't have. A deep passion and a forever kind of love.

"Have you seen Angel?" she asked. "That stubborn dog hasn't come to my calls."

"No." Lucia's voice filled with concern as she moved to stand beside her at the window. "Has she been gone all day?"

Emma nodded, the worry gnawing at her. "She's usually back by now. She'd better come home soon, before—"

"I'll find her," Lucia assured her, patted her on the arm, then walked back to the stove and opened the oven door. She put on her mitts, and took the roast out of the oven.

Part of Emma knew it was foolish to worry. Angel often ran off in the late afternoon. The silly dog would catch a scent of some rabbit or squirrel, and off she would go, chasing it through the countryside. Always before, she'd come home by dark. Tonight wouldn't be any different, she thought, trying to reassure herself as the sun sank below the horizon.

Only, before now, the dog had always returned when she'd called for her. The scars set deep in her cheek burned. She touched them, rubbing gently.

"Is the pain getting worse?" Lucia asked, the worry back in her eyes.

Emma nodded. "It always does this time of year." And not because of the cooler days and nights, as Dr. Callahan liked to say, but because it marked the return of the Equinox, of the wolves, of hopelessness.

"I'll make the salve," Lucia muttered. "In the meantime, take this tray up to your father, but don't let him see your fear." She ladled a hefty serving of potatoes and carrots onto a plate.

Emma pulled her fingers from the jagged edges of the scar tissue. "I know. Dr. Callahan told me to keep him calm. I won't upset him." She took the tray, and walked upstairs to her father's room. For a moment, she stood outside his door, trying to compose herself. She didn't want him worrying about her. Not now, not when his heart was so weak.

She took a deep breath, then walked in with the tray holding his dinner and medications balanced in her hands. "Ready for supper, Dad?"

"Emma," he said, his eyes narrowing as he smiled at her. "Have you been avoiding me?"

"Don't be silly. Why would I be avoiding my favorite dad?"

"Oh, do you have another dad I don't know about?"

She grinned and placed the tray on his lap. "Lucia's made pork roast with carrots and new potatoes. She's really outdone herself tonight."

"You should have brought a tray for yourself and eaten with me," he said, and gave a small pout.

"I should have, you're right," she agreed, reluctant to tell him she couldn't eat. How could she, with her stomach all tied up in knots? She busied herself turning up his light to chase the shadows back into the room's deep corners, then sat in the Queen Anne chair next to the bed.

He took a bite of the meat and chewed thoughtfully. "The Cadre called again today."

Emma stilled as her heart tensed in her chest. "And you talked with them?"

"They were very persuasive."

"I'm sure they were last time, too, and look how that turned out. Mum is dead." The bitterness in her voice almost choked her. The Cadre, an organization that for centuries had protected people from evil, had promised to protect her mother against the curse plaguing their family. Instead the agent they'd sent had ignited the flames that killed them both.

She would have continued railing about the injustice of losing her mum when she was so young, and how she blamed the Cadre for it, but the sadness filling her father's face made her stop. "I'm sorry." She hated to see him looking so lost and vulnerable.

His gray-blue eyes caught hers. "It's not good for us to be living out here all alone. I couldn't bear it if anything happened to you, too."

She forced a conciliatory smile. "That's why nothing will."

"I think we should take them up on their offer and move to St. Yve Manor. We can start a new life there. You can meet people, go to school, make friends."

A ripple of fear shimmered through her heart at the thought. "Wolvesrain is our home. I—"

"This isn't a home," he insisted. "It's a foxhole where we've both been hiding for far too long."

Emma stood and walked toward the window that faced the long drive stretching in front of the house. She heard him set down his knife and fork and push away the tray.

"I love you, Emma, but we both know I'm not going to live much longer. I need to see you settled before I go. The Cadre can help you."

"I can't leave," she said, her voice breaking. She hated to hear him talk this way. She wanted to appease him, but they'd tried before. She left once when he'd sent her to boarding school. Nightmares had plagued her sleep, but worse were the days when she'd been tormented by the taunts of the other students, because she was different and didn't fit in, because of her face.

Rage, forever simmering below the surface, surged within her. "I can't go through that again. Not to mention the curse. I'm better off here away from—"

"Don't even say it. There is no curse. I've told you time and time again. What happened to you and your mother was a horrible tragedy. Not a curse."

She turned and faced him. "Wolves attacked us,

Daddy. Without provocation. Wolves that aren't even supposed to exist in England. And now they're back, can't you hear them?"

"Did you call Animal welfare? The RSPCA?"

"Of course! They say there are no wolves. They can't find them. Nor any sign of them. They think I'm insane—the poor daft woman who's spent too much time locked up in her old crumbling manor." Her hands clenched into fists at her side.

"I'm sorry for that, but that doesn't mean there's a curse, it just means they're not very good at their jobs."

"They're right! There are no wolves. They're demons, called by some jilted gypsy two hundred years ago to rain terror down on our family."

"Don't you hear how ridiculous you sound? This family is not cursed. Now I don't want to hear any more about it, is that clear?" Her father's face flushed as he said the words, and he started to cough and wheeze.

Emma sucked in a breath and rushed forward. "Daddy?" She knew better than to upset him. She grabbed a glass off the bedside table and filled it with water, then handed it to him.

He took the glass, then waved her away as he took a long drink. "I'm okay, really."

Relieved, she dropped into the chair next to the bed. She knew better than to bring it up. But she was the one who'd seen her mother die. She was the one who'd heard her last words. *Don't ever succumb to love, Emma. Promise me.*

The howling started again, creating a nasty racket.

Emma blinked back the burning in her eyes and the bitterness in her throat. She stood and once more returned to the window. "They've been coming closer and closer to the house lately," she whispered, as a rash of shivers puckered her skin, prickling the three deep gashes cut through her face.

A figure on horseback moved out from behind a cluster of trees and looked up at the house. Her breath caught in her throat and she quickly stepped back from the window.

"I know you're afraid," her father said. "It's almost the Equinox. As soon as that bloody night passes, they'll leave again. They always do. And then things can get back to normal."

"Yes. Normal," she murmured.

"Until then, just to be safe—"

"I know. I won't leave the house." She couldn't even if she wanted to, even if she did have somewhere to go.

"Enjoy your supper, Dad." She turned on the television to the evening news and left the room. She wasn't up to a long visit with him, not tonight.

"Emma?" he said, stopping her.

She turned back. "When he comes, don't turn the Cadre agent away."

She closed her eyes, and tamped down on her growing frustration, then nodded. She might have to invite him in, but that didn't mean she had to talk with him.

Damien Hancock's heart skipped a beat as the woman stepped up to the window. She peered through the glass, looking at him as if she could see him, her blue eyes melting in loneliness. For a moment, he stared at her, moved by her loveliness, by her need. And then she was gone.

He shook off the strange feeling and looked around him, wondering why his brother would have come back here. This was where they'd lost their families, their lives, their humanity. He would have been happy never to have stepped foot near Wolvesrain again. The sooner he found his brother, the sooner he could leave. He reached with his senses, searching for Nicholai's distinct aura, but found nothing.

He'd kept track of his brother's comings and goings through the years. He knew the choices he'd made, the demons he'd fought and fed off. But he'd never looked for him, never wanted to see for himself the monster the Cadre had said Nicholai had become.

Until now.

Damien was tired of hiding, of burying his head in the sand. It was time he faced the truth of who his brother was, what he was. Maybe then he could discover a little something about himself, and what he wanted to do now that he'd cut his ties with the Cadre.

A deer stepped out from behind a bush and froze. The forest was full of the sounds he recalled from his youth, the smell of the beast, the deep dank richness of the earth. How could he be here and not remember the way it used to be?

He looked at the old manor house, with its dark oaks winding their limbs toward the dusty windows. The rotting shingles, the rusted iron. Nothing of its former grandeur. The thought pleased him. He'd like nothing better than to see Wolvesrain burn to the ground.

Before he could think on it further, the deer scampered off, and the large black stallion tramped the ground beneath its feet. He clucked his tongue and the horse moved slowly forward. It hadn't gone more than ten yards when it stopped and backed up nervously, its ears twitching, the scent of fear rolling off it in thick waves.

Then he heard the sounds of something racing toward him. The horse neighed in alarm, its ears flattening, its nostrils flaring. It rose up on its hind legs, almost knocking Damien to the ground.

"All right, boy. All right," he cajoled.

The horse reared again, its heart pounding against its ribcage beneath Damien's tensed thighs. He turned the horse around, leaned forward, and kicked it into movement, tightening his calves, sending the horse away from Wolvesrain.

As they reached the cover of the trees once more, he turned back, looking toward the manor house. Wolves were racing toward them, their eyes gleaming red in the distance. He counted four, too many even for his superior strength.

Asmos's demon wolves here for the woman in the window. Here to fulfill a gypsy curse. And then he knew why his brother was here. He was targeting the demon. His sights were set high this time. Too high.

The leather strap that had kept Damien's hair bound

at his nape loosened, and long strands of black hair fell free as the horse's muscles moved taut and strong beneath him. He turned away from Wolvesrain and rode deeper into the forest as night cloaked him in darkness

He urged his horse faster, racing through the forest, searching for the presence that had teased him since he first arrived back in this part of England.

His brother, Nicholai.

In the distance a faint glow peeked through the trees, growing brighter as he approached the clearing. His pulse raced quicker, his body heat rising. He could smell the blood of the forest animals scurrying away from him, could hear it pulsing through the horse's strong body beneath him.

But it was the village beckoning in the distance, not a clan of demon-feeding vampires. A good ten minutes later, Damien slowed the horse to a trot, then a walk. The poor beast was drenched with sweat and fear. Damien opened his mind, searching the area around him for the wolves. They were nowhere around. Neither was Nicholai.

Emma started down the back staircase, but hesitated as a familiar scent wafted on the air. Slowly, she continued down the stairs, her hand grasping hold of the rail while her mind groped for the source of the scent.

"Lucia?" she called, and stopped on the bottom step as her heart kicked up a nervous beat. Her gaze locked on to the panel door to the cellar that, when closed, was set flush into the far wall of the kitchen. Only now it was cracked open. Anxiety squeezed her heart.

She lifted a leaden foot and stepped to the kitchen floor. She supposed she'd known the door was there, set so well into the woodwork that one had to look closely in order to see the seams, but it had been so long since she'd actually thought on it, since she'd seen it open. Dread's icy fingers skittered up her spine.

She couldn't take her gaze off the door, and yet, her eyes ached from staring at it, from knowing that at any moment the door would swing open wider and she'd be able to see into the darkness beyond.

Her heart pounded so hard her chest hurt. She rubbed the area between her breasts, trying to soothe the ache as a dull roar thundered in her ears. She stepped closer. She didn't want to see what was down there. What she wanted was to turn and run, to put as much distance between herself and the cellar as she possibly could.

Instead, she moved toward the door that led into the rear yard. She reached for the glass knob, as the familiar scent still drifted through her mind. Buried memories teased her, threatening to come to the surface.

She'd opened the cellar door before. Vaguely, she remembered steps that shifted and groaned beneath her feet. She recalled this same overly sweet scent, and the darkness, a deep, inky black that ate up every speck of light. She hadn't even been able to see her fingers in front of her. And something else had been down there, something that hovered just out of reach.

Why couldn't she remember? She glanced back at

the cellar door. Why was she so afraid, so certain that if she went down there again, she wouldn't come back? What had happened down there? She thought harder, letting her mind drift back down those stairs.

She remembered smoke rising from candles, from incense. She remembered shadows shifting on the wall, and something moving across the floor. Something dark and oozing. Blood. High-pitched screams reverberated through her mind. A child's screams. Her screams.

Fear, thick and pulsing, stole her breath.

*Run, Emma.*

She yanked open the back door and ran out into the night away from her memories, away from that sickly sweet scent. She stopped halfway across the yard, and leaned against a tree, her fingers digging into the hard bark. A cool breeze caressed her face, lifting her hair, and soothing her fevered skin. The moon was full, lighting the yard, casting a silvery glow on the forest's tall trees. Beckoning her forward.

Her eyes drifted shut. Images whirled through her mind. Blood…rivers of it, rushing across the floor, seeping into the cracks in the stones, flowing toward her, covering her feet. She gasped and opened her eyes. Something moved, coming toward her. A blur raced across the corner of her vision.

"Angel," she called her dog, her voice sounding pathetically weak. But she knew better. She knew what was out there. She heard the panting, loud and rasping, too loud for her sweet little Angel. She turned and saw what her mind would never let her forget—gleaming wolf eyes flashing red in the wan light. Her heart stopped.

A scream gurgled in her throat. She knew she should run, but she couldn't make herself move.

"Emma!" Lucia cried from behind her. She grabbed Emma's arm, yanking her back across the yard and into the kitchen then slammed and locked the door behind them. "You can't go out there. You know that!" Lucia's eyes were wild with fear, as her strong fingers dug painfully into Emma's shoulders. "What were you doing out there? You can't do that again."

"I know. I'm sorry," Emma said and tried to twist free. "I just had to get away." She looked past Lucia at the opened cellar door.

Lucia let go and took a quick step back, her chest rising and falling as she struggled to control her breathing.

Emma rubbed the sting out of her shoulders. "I was just calling Angel," she lied, and scrubbed her face with her hands. "I'm fine. I'm okay. I won't do it again."

Lucia nodded, and visibly tried to calm herself.

"Really," Emma insisted and forced herself to smile. "I'm sorry. I'll be more careful." She shook a brittle laugh loose from her chest, but before she could chase away the last vestiges of fear, a loud crash hit the side of the house, shaking the room, rattling the glass.

Lucia gasped. Emma jumped back as a large gray wolf peered through the window.

The first to react, Lucia ran toward it, waving her arms above her head. "Get out of here!" she cried.

Emma stood frozen to the spot as the wolf's eyes

locked on hers. The beast opened its mouth and crinkled its nose, baring long, vicious fangs, its mouth lifting in a snarl.

"He's come for me," Emma said softly.

"Get away," Lucia screamed, grabbing a broom from the corner and swinging it at the window.

The wolf stared for another long moment, then turned and walked away.

Emma collapsed into a chair and rubbed at the scars burning like liquid fire in her flesh. "Maybe Dad is right. Maybe we should get out of here."

"We're not going anywhere," Lucia said, her voice hardening as her eyes filled with distress. "They won't let us."

Behind her, the door to the cellar yawned open, and, as Emma peered into the darkness beyond, a cold certainty seeped through her bones that Lucia was right. They couldn't leave. The wolves wouldn't let them. She had no choice. No hope. She was… *cursed*.

# Chapter 2

Damien Hancock's blood rushed through his system toward his center. His teeth sharpened. He was filled to bursting with need—for food, for sex. And not necessarily in that order. He groaned as he smelled the sweet perfume of Anna, the cleaning girl, as she worked in the rooms upstairs. The throbbing in his groin intensified.

He heard the faint heartbeat of a rodent hidden behind the wall and his stomach turned with an intense need to feed.

There were several bags of bovine blood chilled in the room where he slept, but he couldn't stomach the thought of them. He wanted warm blood. Fresh blood. Human blood? He closed his eyes and took a deep breath, focusing on steadying himself, his fingers stroking the crystal in his pocket.

He took the amber-colored quartz out of his pocket and stared into its center, using his power to slow his heartbeat to a steady rhythm, to will his muscles to relax. His thirst mellowed. He walked toward the fridge, opened the door and tore open a bag of blood and drank greedily, then closed his eyes and deepened his breathing.

As a long-time member of the Cadre, he'd learned how to hone his self-discipline and use his power to strengthen his control. Only through self-denial and years of training had he become sufficiently worthy to be an adept—a master of the occult, a demon hunter. Someone worthy of capturing demons and returning them to the Cadre for interrogation, then, if warranted, for deportation to the demon realm.

It was because of his work to become an adept that he'd never touched a drop of human blood. That denial made him stronger, made him pure of heart and able to battle those who weren't and win. But that didn't make him crave the blood any less.

His phone rang, chiming through the walls and sending dread straight to his gut. He walked back down the corridor and into a sealed room, closing and locking the door behind him. Only one person had this number, only one person who'd bother to call. He stepped up to a videophone and pushed the button. "Hello, Nica."

Nica Burrows, Communications Director at the Cadre, had been giving him his assignments for a long time and, as much as he might try, refused to let him gracefully fade away. The woman was tenacious, and annoyed the hell out of him.

"Hello, Damien. How are you faring?"

"Well, thank you," he lied. He always lied to the Cadre now. No reason to bare his soul to them. They were all about what was best for the Cadre, and to hell with what was best for him or anyone else. Which was exactly why he'd cut his ties with them, if only they would leave them cut.

"Is that blood on your chin?" she asked.

Once again he was reminded why he hated modern technology. "Sorry, pet. Just had breakfast."

No expression entered her picture-perfect face. She might as well have been a wax doll—all ash-blond hair, glassy blue eyes and porcelain skin. He couldn't even recall her scent, probably because the blood that ran through her veins was ice-cold.

"We're picking up strange readings at Wolvesrain," Nica said. "Since you're back in England, and you're familiar with the area, with Wolvesrain, we thought you might be interested in helping us with this one small matter."

He smiled, one corner of his mouth lifting. "Small matter? There is nothing small about Asmos."

She arched one perfect brow. "Yes, and it is close to the Equinox. But the readings are stronger than usual. Something is happening out there. The demon wolves are back, and they're stronger than before. You used to live there, Damien, before."

"You mean when I was human?"

"You knew the McGovern ancestor, Amelia, who was cursed by the gypsy," she continued.

"True." He wouldn't deny it. Camilla had been part of his clan. He knew she was powerful, he just had no idea she would have been able to call on a demon and start a chain of events that was still causing him trouble to this day.

"The McGoverns are scared. They need our help. With you right there, who better to end this? Who better than you to be there to send Asmos back where he came from?"

She had a point. It would be almost like starting over. And wasn't that exactly what he wanted? A fresh start? To answer to no one but himself? To set out on a journey to learn the true purpose of why he was here?

"Just bring Emma to us where she'll be safe. Then you can pick up the demon containment stones to use on Asmos. It's what you've been trained for. It's what you're good at."

"And you trust me with his capture? Come on, Nica. Why call me? Why should I care? Why should I ever want to capture another demon again after what happened last time?" After his complete failure?

Nica closed her eyes and when she opened them again, the glassy indifference was gone, replaced by the watery, brittle sheen of pain. "Because we can't risk losing another agent to this demon. This time we need someone special, Damien. Someone like you."

"And what makes me so special?" he asked, trying not to choke on the bitterness filling his mouth. "It wasn't that long ago that I was persona non grata at St. Yve."

"We know you'll be able fight the curse where others have failed."

"Why? Because human blood doesn't pump through my heart? You think that will make me immune to the curse? Immune to the pull toward the McGovern girl?" He thought of the woman he'd seen standing in the window. How lovely she was, how lonely. Just thinking of her standing there started a fire in his belly he was certain wouldn't be easily put out. No, his lack of human blood didn't make him immune to her or the curse. "Maybe it's because you think the girl could never love *someone* like me."

"No, Damien," she said quickly, too quickly. "The point is, even if the worst happens and you succumb to that pull and Emma does fall in love with you, if she does become a vessel for Asmos as her mother did, you will still be able to stop her. She won't be able to kill you as easily as her mother killed Charles Lausen."

Then he remembered, and his mouth went dry. "Charles Lausen was your father, wasn't he?"

She stared at him, her gaze once again turning hard and cold—the chink in her armor sealed.

"If you won't do it for us, do it for Emma McGovern."

He almost laughed out loud. "Emma is the last in Amelia's line, isn't she? Once she's gone, the Cadre will have nothing left to worry about. The curse will be complete."

"She's been marked by the wolves. She has been selected to be the next vessel for Asmos. If he wins, if he possesses her, who knows the damage he could do?"

"Sorry, pet. Not playing this time."

"Please, Damien. At least go to Wolvesrain. Meet the McGoverns, scope out the situation for yourself, then make your decision. All we're asking you to do is to deliver the girl to St. Yve."

"No, you're asking me to go back to Wolvesrain." Back to the place where he'd been reborn. That night, a large clan of vampires had converged on the area, looking for Asmos, looking for Camilla. This particular band of vampires were demon hunters, feeding on possessed victims and familiars, growing stronger with each sip of the demon's essence.

He and his brother had survived that night, to become demon hunters themselves. Damien, however, hunted for the Cadre, while Nicholai did it for the rush, the power, the surge of strength.

"Damien, what concerns us right now is the readings of vampires in the area." Nica's mouth tightened. "We think they're after Asmos's essence. They're after the wolves, and if they find out about Emma, she won't stand a chance. We're sending a containment team. This family has been through hell. How many more people have to die because of this demon?"

Damien sighed and ran tense fingers through his hair. Did he really have any choice? Could he in good conscience turn his back on this one? No, it hit too close to home. He'd spent a good portion of his youth in the forest outside Wolvesrain. He knew the players. Worse, he knew the game. "All right. I'll do it, Nica, but I'm doing it my way."

"Which means?"

"Hold off on the vampire containment team until I get the lay of the land."

"You think you know who they are?" she asked.

"Perhaps." He disconnected the line and turned away before she could see the concern in his eyes. Vampires who drank demon blood were relentless and brutal, and lived on the edge of madness. Unfortunately, he already knew who the leader of this particular pack was.

Who said you could never go home?

Damien revved the engine, tearing up the road in his top-of-the-line black Mercedes CLK55 convertible. He loved to crank this baby up and fly through the countryside with the night wind whipping through his long hair. He turned the bend and flew down the long gravel road flanked on either side by old beech trees, and let out a raucous roar. There were few things left in his life that could fill his chest to bursting with absolute joy. One of the downfalls of immortality—everything just becomes so damned mundane.

Beyond the trees, the old forest encroached like soldiers waiting to reclaim their land. He pulled to a quick stop on the cobblestone drive circling in front of Wolvesrain. Impressive in its Gothic Revival architecture, the house, built in the eighteenth century, was several stories of light stone with peaked towers on each wing.

Back when he was young, it had been the most extraordinary estate in the area. The Earl of Wolvesrain generated fear and respect across the shire, while Amelia, his daughter, had been every man's dream.

At that time, Damien had looked upon Wolvesrain with longing and envy. Now, as he took in the rot and decay, all he felt was disgust. He would do as the Cadre asked. He would check out the situation, and determine how much of a threat Asmos really was. Then, he would seek out these vampires, and find out where they'd come from, what they were after, and hope they weren't here for the demon essence. Or the McGovern girl.

As he stepped out of the car, he couldn't help but notice the disrepair of the old house, the crumbling stone, the decaying wood. One of the carriage lights flanking the steps was out, the other barely shone through the dirtied, thick glass. "The old man must be turning over in his grave," he muttered, and chuckled.

A difficult man, the Earl hadn't thought much of the gypsies, and had enjoyed running them off his land with his vicious dogs and cruel threats. One night in particular, when it had been pouring, the children in the camp had been crying from lack of sleep and not much food at supper to fill their swollen bellies, and still the old man had set his dogs on them. His peals of laughter had echoed through the night.

And Nica thought he should care what happened to Wolvesrain and the Earl's descendents? He swallowed a bitter laugh. This place could burn to the ground and he'd bring out the marshmallows for a toasting. He didn't owe Nica or the Cadre anything.

*So why was he here?* The question mocked him. Was it only because of his own kind? Or was it Asmos? Did he want answers from the vampires? Or did he miss the thrill of the hunt, the exhilaration of the capture? Or was he just hoping to find some kind of meaning for his miserable life?

He looked up at the old house, and the forest beyond. This was where it had all started. Where a young gypsy lost her heart, and called up a powerful, primitive demon. Then the vampires had come, wanting a piece of Camilla and her demon, and all hell had broken loose.

Damien's parents had found him lying in the carnage of their camp and had whisked him to the Cadre, hoping for a magical cure to the vampire's bite. Of course, there hadn't been one. And while he might have been reborn that night, his two younger sisters had been viciously mutilated, and his brother? Left to join their maker's clan.

Damien moved toward the house, then stopped as the bushes rustled behind him. It was then that he became aware of the peculiar absence of sounds around him. He reached with his vampire senses, searching for the soft playful tread of deer, or the quick furtive movements of rabbits, but there were none. No animals as far as his mind could touch.

A forest empty of life? Asmos must be near. Damien stared into the night, grasping with his heightened senses, searching for the demon wolves, easily seeing through the dark, but there was nothing. And yet a faint odor circled him—burning brimstone. The air thickened and chilled, moving tangibly across his skin. He stilled.

A lone gray wolf stepped out from behind a tree, its eyes glowing a vibrant red. Then another moved to his right, and yet another to his left. He knew without looking there'd be one more behind him. They stared at him, and he wondered if there was any of the wolf left in them, if they remembered him from a time when both he and Camilla were young and filled with foolish human dreams.

But he knew better. Camilla's pets had become vessels for Asmos to enter the mortal realm and fulfill the wishes of a heartbroken gypsy by carrying out a centuries-old curse one last time. One by one the wolves sat, lifted their noses to the sky and howled homage to their master, Asmos, the demon of wrath.

Soundlessly, Damien stepped past them, walking toward the house and up the stone front steps. He lifted the brass knocker on what appeared to be a massive, impenetrable front door and let it fall. Deep ragged scratches marred the wood in several places. Claw marks.

A gypsy woman opened the door and Damien almost laughed out loud at the irony, at what the old Earl would be thinking of that one! Her midnight-black eyes filled with fear and grew large in her face as she stared at him. Did she know what he was?

"What do you want?" she asked, and pulled the door close to her, blocking his view of the inside of the house.

"Damien Hancock," he said, and offered his hand. "The Cadre sent me to see Miss Emma McGovern."

The woman's lips parted slightly as surprise and indecision warred across her face. She ignored his outstretched hand, and reluctantly stepped back, inviting him in. He shrugged and walked past her, taking in the majesty of the grand marble-floored foyer. He'd always wondered what the inside of this house looked like. She gestured for him to go into the great room, then turned and left without speaking a word.

Surreptitiously, he watched her go. A gypsy who dabbled in the arts—he could tell by the scent of sage and a hint of honeysuckle drifting from her clothing. She had appeared to know instantly what he was, and still she'd invited him in. Interesting.

He entered a circular room with pale-blue silk-covered walls lined with paintings and aged photographs of past inhabitants—an impressive monument to Wolvesrain Manor. A large painting of a woman atop a beautiful snow-white horse commanded the room. *Amelia.*

She, like her father, had been mean-spirited and nasty to the entire gypsy camp. How he'd hated them both. Perhaps it was poetic justice that she should have survived Camilla's wrath to produce a long lineage of tortured heirs burdened by a curse.

And Nica thought he should care.

He stifled a bitter laugh. He'd be curious to see if the current lady of the household was as self-centered and cold-hearted as Amelia had been. He recalled the way

Amelia used to sneer down her nose at him and his friends, believing her lily-white porcelain skin to be too good for them. She thought the gypsy's olive shade was…what was the word she used? Oh, yes—hideous.

Giving a little torment back to the current *lady* of the house might be worth his trouble. He grinned and continued his perusal, stopping to study a painting of the Earl. In this one he looked much older than Damien remembered, and a tad bit sickly.

He heard a movement in the corridor and turned toward the sound of swishing silk skirts and the shuffle of soft satin slippers. A woman stepped into the doorway, graced in layer upon layer of light-green chiffon. His breath caught. Darkness hovered around the furthermost edge of his vision. His chest constricted, palms dampened.

*Isn't she ravishing? Look at the fire burning in the eyes, the soft ruby dewiness of her lips—a peach ripe for the picking. Take a bite, Damien.*

"Beautiful," he agreed, watching the woman sashay into the room, her flaxen hair piled high on her head, a few tendrils escaping to curl down the long column of her exquisite throat. Fire burned in his belly, and he had an overwhelming urge to kiss that throat, to run his tongue gently across her beautiful skin, then sink his teeth deep into her flesh, filling his mouth with her sweet, warm blood.

He licked his lips and felt his fangs descend. Yes, he could almost taste her.

"Mr. Hancock? Are you all right?" A soft voice

broke through the cloud in his mind, interrupting his delicious thoughts.

Stunned, he turned to the side and placed a hand over his mouth and pretended to cough until his teeth moved back to their rightful place. His stomach turned. Where had these thoughts—these desires—come from? He'd known the curse would try and draw him toward her, but could Camilla's curse really be this strong? He sucked in a deep breath and steadied himself.

"Mr. Hancock?" Miss McGovern said again, her lilting voice warm and gentle like the caress of butterfly wings upon his cheek. He turned back and looked at her face—her flawless skin, her cherry lips ready for the tasting, her sky-blue eyes fresh and wide-open like the morning horizon beckoning a new day. "Are you all right? You're as white as a ghost." She reached her hand toward his.

He took it in his own and stared down at creamy white skin and marveled at the gentleness of her touch, the silky feel of her skin against his. His blood quickened. *No,* he answered in his mind, *not a ghost, but a vampire.* A beast who would love to take just a small sip.

"I'm fine," he choked. "Emma McGovern?" He had to get hold of himself. He felt as if he had no control of his thoughts, of his senses, of his actions. He took another deep breath. Nonsense. He was Damien. Adept. Master of the occult. He'd trained for many years, honing his focus, his control. He would not fall victim to a foolish gypsy girl's curse.

"Yes." Miss McGovern looked at him quizzically, and with concern widening her beautiful eyes. "Welcome to Wolvesrain."

"Thank you," he muttered, and cleared his throat as he tried to grasp hold of the powerful sensations coursing through him. He forced a smile to put her at ease.

She turned and he noticed with a mind-wrenching jolt that she wasn't wearing a gown, as he'd first thought, but blue jeans. Nor was her long golden hair piled up on her head, but instead it hung loose. In fact, she kept her head tilted so it hung in front of one side of her face, covering…something.

What kind of magic could alter his perceptions so completely? As he looked closer, a wave of dizziness swept over him, and the twinkling of laughter whispered through his mind. Asmos, a *Daemon Incultus,* more primitive and powerful than anything he had ever run across. No wonder the Cadre had sent him. Charles Lausen hadn't stood a chance against a demon curse this strong.

Damien only hoped he did.

## Chapter 3

"Lucia," Emma called, her sing-song voice echoing through the room. "Mr. Hancock needs some hot tea and biscuits."

The gypsy seemed to appear from nowhere to glower at him. Apparently, she'd been hovering. Annoyance surged through Damien, tensing his shoulders and, for a second, he imagined following her into the kitchen and taking a deep bite off that old gypsy neck.

Horrified by the thought, he slipped his hand into his pocket and wrapped it around the crystal, rubbing his thumb over the sharpest point, and focused on finding his center, his strength. He'd never once tasted human blood. That decision to remain pure, to fight his urges and focus on enhancing his power of control had made him what he was—a master adept, and the best demon hunter the Cadre had.

But he no longer worked for the Cadre, and he'd never faced a force as strong as this curse. He didn't know how much worse these feelings could get. All he knew was that if he didn't wrestle some control over his urges, this family could add him to their list of things to worry about.

"Please sit," Emma said, and gestured to the settee in the middle of the room.

He nodded, and moved toward the couch. The light-headedness wouldn't cease, nor the play on his perceptions, and the deep need in his gut. He inhaled, closing his eyes and concentrated on his breathing. Just when he thought he had himself under control, the scent of lavender swirled through his mind.

*It's the blood, Damien. You need the blood. Her blood.*

He opened his eyes and Emma was staring at him, a look of worry lining her beautiful face. She looked so fragile, so vulnerable, a fierce need to protect her swept through him as easily as a fire burning across a dry field.

He started to assure her that he was fine, that she would be okay, that he was there to help her, but then his gaze dropped to the lace of her blouse gently brushing against her throat. A small vein hidden beneath her delicate skin pulsed. He yearned to touch it with the tip of his tongue, to taste her soft, supple skin. He shifted closer, his breath going shallow.

Lucia walked quickly into the room, carrying a large tray of tea and biscuits, and dropped it on the walnut table in front of them with a bang. She poured the tea and thrust a cup at him.

"Thank you," he murmured, then brought the cup to his lips, and gave her a twisted smile over the rim. She huffed indignantly, then turned away. The woman was too aware for her own good.

"So, how does the Cadre think they can help us this time?" Emma asked, as she sipped her tea.

*They can't.* He bit down on his immediate response. He paused, trying to refocus, but suddenly didn't care. He stared at her, willing her to turn and look at him. He yearned to lose himself once more in those incredible cornflower-blue eyes.

She continued to sip her tea, which kept her from having to turn fully to look at him. In fact, she'd hardly looked at him at all. What was she hiding beneath all that hair? He watched the light glimmer and bounce off the shiny strands, and for the first time in many years, felt the thrill of the unknown pump through his veins. This house was full of mysteries, of excitement, of danger.

*Think how that long, silky hair would feel brushing against your bare skin, so soft, so gentle.*

Yes. A part of him welcomed the unbidden thoughts as he watched the movement of those long, blond strands and suddenly he yearned to touch them, to reach over and brush her hair off her face. To run it through his fingers and wrap it behind the curve of her ear, baring her neck to his gentle touch. Just thinking of the things he wanted to do to her, and wanted her to do to him, made him stiffen beneath the supple leather of his pants. He shifted, trying to find comfort.

"The last time the Cadre sent someone to Wolves-rain to 'help,' it didn't turn out so well," she added, her voice hardening.

"I've heard," he said, shifting again. "They think I'm...different."

"Are you?" She straightened and looked in his eyes. Fear emanated from her, so strong he could almost taste it. And something else. *Anger.*

He breathed deep, sucking it in. "You don't have to be afraid." He could take care of her. Protect her. Angry red marks peeked out from beneath her hair. "May I?" he asked, and slowly reached toward her.

She stiffened as he gently lifted her hair back from her face.

Anger took root and spread within him as he took in the three deep gashes marring her beautiful skin. But even the anger didn't diminish his need to touch her, and to have her touch him. "What happened?" he rasped, and clenched a fist at his side.

"Wolf attack, when I was a child."

He thought of the scratches on the door and cringed, knowing they would come for her again, knowing the wolves were outside now, waiting. And she was so vulnerable.

*Protect her, Damien. You're all she has.*

He stood and turned away from her, fighting the

voice he knew was Asmos. Fighting the desire to pull her into his arms and make love to her, to chase away her fear. Knowing that was exactly what the demon wanted.

He turned back to face her. "The Cadre would like you to come with me to St. Yve. You will be protected there, and even better, they can show you how to protect yourself."

"Protect myself from what?" she asked, her eyes probing his. The howling started again. She shuddered, then stood and approached the French doors.

"They're not just wolves," he said, absently, trying desperately to focus on the situation, on what he needed to say to convince her. But her fear was almost palpable, almost audible as it rushed through her blood.

*Intoxicating, isn't it, Damien? Think how fast her blood is pumping through her veins. So sweet. Just one sip, what would it hurt? If you did it right, she won't even know. In fact, she'll enjoy it.*

Just one taste? Damien's sharpened fangs descended. He stepped behind her, his hand brushing her shoulder. He leaned close, breathing deeply of her sweet lavender scent. Her skin was so soft, so delicate.

"Emma, you look tired," Lucia said, as she walked into the room. "Go upstairs, take a hot bath, and call it a night. I'll look after your dad and—" she gestured toward Damien with a look of disgust twisting her face "—him."

Damien stepped back and turned toward the hearth. Had he really almost bitten her? Two hundred and fifty years without once sipping human blood, and he'd almost succumbed after less than thirty minutes in this house? Camilla's curse, Asmos's machinations, were proving too powerful, even for him.

"Mr. Hancock?" Emma started.

"Damien, please," he responded, turning back to her. As he looked into her cornflower-blue eyes, he was once again struck by her beauty, by the soft, gentle way she spoke and moved. Hunger coiled within him.

"It's late, and I haven't offered you anything to eat—"

*Look how her skin glows in the soft light, look at her lips, so plump, so ripe.*

Oh, yes. His gaze fixed on the soft rhythm of her pulse, clearly evident beneath her luminescent skin. His teeth ached.

"Are you hungry?"

*Starved.* He shook his head. "Sorry?"

"Can I offer you some supper?"

"No." He took a step back. "Thank you. I've already eaten." He had to get hold of himself. For the first time, he wasn't sure if he could control this…*bloodlust.*

He'd always thought he'd had an understanding of the term, but he'd been wrong. Now he knew. "I understand that you don't want to leave your home, but St. Yve really would be a better place for you right now." For both of them. He couldn't stay here any longer than she could.

Her jaw stiffened and she pulled back, once again re-treating behind her hair. "How would you or the Cadre know what would be better for me?"

He stepped forward and grasped hold of her chin, forcing her to look at him. "Trust me. I know more than you can imagine."

She gasped, and jerked away from his touch.

"I think you should leave," Lucia demanded.

"I'm sorry." He moved away from Emma, annoyed that he even cared what the wolves had done to her. What Asmos had planned for her next. She was the Earl's blood. Amelia's blood!

*Can't you hear it rushing through her delicate veins?*

Damien stiffened, nervousness bunching his muscles. He had to get out of this house. He was the last person the Cadre should have sent to *help* her. He felt the curse too strongly, felt Asmos as if he were in the room, his essence swirling around him, thick as smoke—black, evil smoke that filled his lungs and infected his thoughts.

"You don't know anything about me," Emma insisted. "How could you? We've never even met before."

He spun round, feeling almost desperate to get her out of this house. "I know you're afraid to go out those front doors. You live in constant fear, fear of the people in the city, and fear of the wolves in the forest. Living your life in hiding is no way to live. It's time for you to make a stand. Come with me."

Emma stared at him. How could he know how she felt? How could he know anything about her after having just met her? Afraid that somehow it was all clear in her eyes, she turned away from him and walked once again toward the French doors. A wolf stepped up to the glass and stared at her. She jumped back, muffling a small cry.

Damien touched her shoulder. She turned and looked up into his steel-blue eyes, and saw they had softened. "It's okay. I'm here to help."

Was it possible? She wanted to believe him, wanted to grasp on to some kind of hope. "Can the Cadre really help us?"

"Don't believe him, Emma," Lucia whispered, her warning reverberating through Emma's mind. Her father asked her to let him in, she had, she was polite. But that didn't mean she had to leave with him. And although he seemed to know a great deal about her, what did she know about him?

She stole a glance at him as he stood in front of the stone hearth, his black hair brushed back off his face, his bright-blue gaze staring at her through dark-rimmed eyes. Thick eyebrows and a strong jawline betrayed strength of character, but it was his deep stare that affected her most. He looked at her as if he knew her, as if he'd always known her.

Emma approached the table, picked up the tea service and handed it to Lucia. She would not go up to bed. She would stay here and discover as much about this man as she could, because he was right about one thing, she had a decision to make. "Don't worry, Lucia, I can handle this."

Lucia started to protest, then stopped as Emma narrowed her eyes. Lucia stiffened her shoulders and left the room. Emma turned back to Damien. His head was tilted as if hearing something, and concern lined his face.

"You can't stay here," he said. "At some point, you're going to have to trust someone to help you. You can't fight Asmos on your own."

"Who's Asmos?"

"The demon who lives in the wolves. The demon who's come to claim you."

She stared at him, unable for a second to comprehend what he was saying. A demon? Fear, cold and sharp, pierced her heart. "But, I thought the curse was about love?"

"Asmos is the demon who will fulfill the curse. He will tempt you to fall in love, whispering in your mind, heightening your awareness, until you feel you will go mad if you don't feel love's touch."

His voice dripped across her senses, even as his words shocked her. What if what he said were true? How could she fight it? How could she protect herself from a demon? But the questions, the fears and doubts, faded as Damien's spicy scent filled her.

Without thought, her gaze dropped to his full lips and she couldn't help wondering, what would they taste like? How would they feel brushed up against hers?

*Do it, Emma. Touch him. Kiss him. He's the one you've been waiting for. The love you've always wanted, but have never had.*

She tried to push the thoughts from her mind, but her head was spinning. Suddenly she wanted him to touch her. She stepped closer to him, even as her mind, her voice found protest. "I can't leave. My father—"

*That's it, Emma. Never leave. Stay here with him. He's been waiting for you, too.*

Damien took her hand in his, and she knew as soon as she felt his touch that the voice was right, they were meant to be together. They'd been waiting so long, and now they'd finally found each other.

"You *can* leave. We'll take your father with us," his voice was soothing, a balm for her aching lonely heart. She listened to him as he whispered through her mind, but she didn't really hear what he was saying. How could she, when his fingers touched her hand, moving softly over her skin, making her feel as if she'd never been touched before?

She looked down at his long, strong fingers. His skin was smooth, his grasp confident. His voice filled her like thick sweet honey fresh from the hive while his mere presence set her body quivering, as if every nerve ending was exposed.

She looked up and searched his eyes for any sign of what he was feeling. Was he feeling this connection between them? Or was revulsion all he felt when looking at her marred face? But what she saw surprised her—admiration, honesty and desire.

*He thinks you're beautiful, Emma.*

Was it possible? His gaze drew her in, pulling her toward him. There was no escape. Her pulse raced and warmth flushed her skin. She imagined what it would be like to touch his raven-black hair, to run her fingers across the darkened stubble along his jawline. What kind of spell had he cast over her? No, not a spell, a curse...a gypsy curse.

*Don't ever succumb to love, Emma. Promise me.* Her mother's pleading words filled her mind. She'd made the promise, but she'd never imagined desire's pull would be so strong. So extreme. And even now, staring into this stranger's feral gaze, she could see the gypsy blood coursing though him, could feel it drawing her in.

She looked down at the floor. She would not give in. She couldn't.

*Go on, Emma. He wants you. Can't you see it? Feel it?* The urgent voice grew louder in her mind, kindling an excitement she'd only dreamed of. Telling her exactly what she wanted to hear, and then she knew it wasn't a voice at all. It couldn't be. It was her wishful thinking. She'd finally gone mad. The alternative? A demon thirsting for her soul.

She pulled free and turned from him. No. She couldn't give in to it now. She was stronger than that, stronger than the evil plaguing her—this demon. This Asmos. She had to be, or surely she would fall victim to the curse herself, and then, like her mother and her mother's mother before her, she would die.

"Why should I trust you?" she asked, her voice breaking because she wanted to trust him. She wanted to believe in him, in hope that there was a way out of this nightmare.

"Because you have no other choice. You're alone out

here. And if you don't listen to me, if you don't come with me to St. Yve, you will not survive the Equinox."

Defiance crept through her. "I've survived the last twenty-five Equinoxes, what makes this one so different? How do I know you're not trying to scare me?"

"You don't need me for that. You're scared enough on your own."

He was dead-on about that, but she wasn't about to admit it to him.

He walked toward the windows. She turned and saw his head once more cocked at the weird angle.

"What is it? Do you hear something?"

He stiffened then turned to her, his blue eyes hardening. "Lock your doors and windows tonight, and don't let anyone else in the house."

"Why, what is it?" she demanded, her nerves already coiled into a tight spring. She didn't need any more surprises. Not tonight.

"I'm not sure," he muttered, and stared out into the darkness. Something about his posture, about the set of his jaw, set her imagination working overtime. "Get a good night's sleep, and think on what I've said. Let your father know we'll be leaving for St. Yve tomorrow evening."

She almost choked. Just like that? Did she have any choice in the matter at all? "I take it you'll be staying then?"

"If that's all right with you?"

She almost snorted. No, it wasn't all right with her. Nothing about any of this was all right with her. The wolves started howling again, sounding much closer than she cared for. She jumped, then hugged herself. All right, she supposed she was glad he was there. Just a little. "Thank you," she said, stiffly. "I'll appreciate having a protector in the house."

As she said the words something shifted in his eyes, making her wonder if perhaps she'd made a mistake. What if Lucia had been right all along? What if the Cadre couldn't be trusted?

She turned toward the staircase. It didn't matter what any of them thought. She had no choice but to trust him. There were no other avenues open to her, no one else who believed she needed help.

No one alive who had ever looked at her the way he did. As if she was worth something. *As if she was… beautiful.*

# Chapter 4

An idiot. A dolt. A lovesick puppy. Emma climbed the stairs to her room, berating herself all the way. Some man gives her a smidgen of attention, and she's ready to fall in line and do whatever it was he wanted of her. How stupid was she?

She walked into her room, shut the door behind her and leaned against the heavy wooden frame. She sighed as she looked around the room, seeing all the things she'd always taken for granted. Her antique four-poster bed with its eyelet-covered duvet, the rocking chair with its thick cushions in the corner next to the window, and the soft blue crocheted blanket her mother had made. Would this be the last night she spent in her home? Would she really do as Damien asked and go with him to St. Yve?

Her gaze fell on the empty dog bed in the corner, and worry blossomed in her chest. Where was Angel? How would she sleep without her dog safe in the room with her? And what if she left? Would Damien let her take Angel with them?

She lit the white candle next to her bed, then walked to the bedroom window and looked out at the moon hanging in the sky. Her gaze searched the grounds behind the house for any sign of the small white dog, but she couldn't see her. Soon it would be the night of the autumn Equinox. If she could just make it through a couple of more days, she'd be safe for another year.

But each year it got worse, the burning in her scars, the threatening presence of the wolves. Did she really want to continue living this way, living in constant fear, marking the passing of time by a single event, year after year?

If it was possible that the Cadre could teach her how to protect herself, could empower her to make her own decisions, her own choices, shouldn't she at least try? Even if it meant leaving Wolvesrain? Her stomach twisted in knots at the thought. She took a deep breath and let her gaze fall on the maze behind the house.

The tall labyrinth had been her family's pride and joy for several generations. When she was only five, they'd moved to Wolvesrain from London. Her mother had been enchanted with the twists and turns of the maze's hedges. They'd spent hours clipping and pruning the swirling design back into shape.

Unfortunately her mum had died before they'd finished. Emma had never stepped foot in it again, but instead watched it fall to ruin night after night from this window. At the maze's center was a large fountain with a cherub pointing its arrow toward the sky. There was no one left to care for it, to love it, except her.

And she was too afraid.

She leaned her forehead against the glass and looked at the family cemetery up on the hill where the plots of her ancestors were overgrown with weeds and vines, the dilapidated tombstones crumbling to dust and decay. In the light of the moon, she could see the large Celtic cross had sunk and was leaning over on its side. Sadness filled her as she thought of her mother buried there beneath the weeds and rotting flowers.

This nightmare had to end. She had to reclaim her life. Even if that meant leaving Wolvesrain and going to St. Yve. Anything had to be better than this. Dropping the curtains, she turned back to her room, picked up a large piece of chalk from the bowl next to the window, and refreshed the outline of the protection circle that surrounded her bed as Lucia had taught her to do. Three times she drew the never-ending line while calling to the goddess Athena to protect her, to let her survive another night without falling victim to the wolf.

Without falling victim to a demon. She shivered. She shouldn't be surprised. The wolves weren't natural, the way they came back year after year. The way their eyes glowed red. Demons from hell. And now hell had a name—Asmos.

She sprinkled salt beneath the door and window, to protect her from evil while she slept. She'd performed the same ritual every night since her mother had died, but she'd never really believed it would help. It certainly had never protected her from her nightmares. But she'd had no other alternative.

Now that she did, would she take it?

She put the chalk back, then let her clothes fall to the ground. Standing naked in the flickering candlelight, she stuck her pinky in olive oil, then drew another protection circle three times across her chest. "Please protect me from the wolves," she murmured. She took a deep breath, then climbed under the soft sheets. "And protect Angel while you're at it, and send her back home."

Her head sank into the soft pillow, and she tried not to think about her dog, or what tomorrow might bring. As she lay there, tossing and turning, swirls of steely-blue darkness filled her mind. Damien's eyes pulled at her, making her lightheaded, disorienting her to the point that all she wanted to do was cling to his strong shoulders, and have him hold and protect her. But would he?

She had to put him out of her mind. But he was just downstairs, and if she quieted her thumping heart, she might be able to hear him. She beat the pillow with her fist, then turned on her side, wishing Angel were there with her.

Would she ever feel the warmth of a man in the bed next to her? Would she ever fall asleep listening to the rhythmic breathing of the one she loved? She sighed, her eyes drifting closed. *Don't ever succumb to love, Emma.* Her mother's voice echoed in her mind bringing a tear to moisten her cheek as she fell into a fitful sleep.

*Emma didn't want to do it. She knew she shouldn't. But she couldn't help herself. She lifted her small foot and stepped onto the narrow staircase. "Mummy?" she called down into the dark cellar, but Mummy didn't answer.*

*She looked back into the kitchen behind her. Maybe she should just go back to bed. She'd heard Mummy get up, and, wanting some water, she'd followed her to the kitchen. Only Mummy didn't stop. She'd hurried down into the cellar, into the dark.*

*Emma clung to the wall, looking down the rickety stairs. There was a lightbulb above her, but it wasn't very bright and didn't reach into the corners. She hated the cellar. Hated going down there. If there were such a thing as trolls, like in the storybooks Lucia read to her, this was where they lived.*

*Her lower lip trembled. She could do this. She and Mummy had been down here before, using the secret passage to get to the maze. But even then, when she'd cling tightly to Mummy's hand, she was certain the darkness was reaching for her.*

*"Mummy?" she called again, louder this time. She heard a strange voice and her mummy laughing. She grabbed hold of the rough rail, careful not to get a splinter and went down the steps.*

*The cellar smelled of onions. She wrinkled her nose. She hated onions, but there was another smell, too. One that smelled worse than onions. One that was yucky.*

*She hesitated only a second before stepping off the rickety boards and onto the dirt floor. Her feet were going to get dirty and Lucia would be mad at her. She followed the sound of her mother's voice, away from the passageway to the maze, past the shelves filled with cans of vegetables and stores of onions, garlic and potatoes and toward another room. A bigger room, where the bad smell grew stronger.*

*Firelight flickered ahead and, holding her hand over her nose, she moved toward it. Shadows crept along the floor, falling across her feet. She stopped and turned, looking around her, but didn't see anything. She sneaked a peek behind her at the hidden alcove beneath the stairs, but no light shone in there at all, and as she stared into the darkness it felt as though something was in there, something…watching her.*

*She whimpered and continued forward, moving toward the murmur of Mummy's voice. She stopped as she entered the next room and gasped. Mummy was kissing Mr. Lausen. She was making strange noises, and he looked like he was squishing her. Worse, neither one of them was wearing their pajamas.*

*"Mummy?" she called, and stepped toward them. A low growl stopped her. She drew in a breath so quickly it hurt. Four wolves were sitting around the room. She knew they were wolves and not just dogs, because she'd seen them on the telly. Only these wolves looked mean.*

They looked like they wanted to bite her. Tears sprang to her eyes.

Her mummy screamed and arched her back. "Mummy!" Emma cried. But Mummy didn't hear her. She had curved her hands, and scraped her nails across Mr. Lausen's back in a vicious swipe. He reared up, a look of pain momentarily crossing his face as his back started to bleed. Then he kissed Mummy again, hard.

Emma stared at the blood running down his back and wondered why he didn't seem to care. She took a small step toward them. Mummy turned her head and looked at Emma, but there was something wrong with her eyes. For a second, they flashed red.

Emma jumped back, hitting her head on the wall behind her. Tears overwhelmed her, running down her face. "Mummy." She hiccupped, and tried to catch her breath. But she couldn't breathe, she couldn't think, and she was so scared.

Mr. Lausen rose, tipped his head back and looked up toward the ceiling, and then roared, his voice thundering through the room.

"Mummmeee!" Emma cried and slid down the wall until she was sitting on the floor. She should run. She knew that, every instinct was telling her to run as fast as she could back up the stairs. But she was too scared to move. Instead, she grabbed her knees to her chest and buried her face within her pajamas.

The smoke from the incense and candles thickened. Her eyes burned, her lungs ached. She wished she were upstairs in her bed with her dolly. She sobbed, crying *for her mummy, for Lucia, for her daddy to come get her and take her away from this awful place.*

*Emma looked up as her mummy screamed. She grabbed Mr. Lausen and picked up a knife lying under a blanket next to her and slashed it across Mr. Lausen's neck. Horrified, Emma stared as blood splattered across the walls in a wide arc.*

*Emma gasped as Mr. Lausen reared back, grabbing his neck with both hands. She watched spellbound as blood dripped to the ground and flowed across the floor, seeping into cracks in the stones.*

*She wanted to turn away, but was afraid that if she did, it would come toward her. Touch her.*

*Without a backward glance, Mummy pushed Mr. Lausen aside and stood. She was naked and dripping with blood. She opened her mouth in a wide, twisted smile, then walked toward Emma.*

*Emma screamed. She tried to push herself backward, but hit the wall again. She scooted sideways trying to get as far from her mother as she could.*

*The wolves stood, howling. Emma cried and, finally able to move, jumped to her feet. She ran toward the other room, toward the stairs and the kitchen, and her bed upstairs.*

*But she never made it that far.*

*"Emma," he mother called, suddenly sounding normal, suddenly sounding like Mummy.*

*Emma stopped with one foot on the bottom step and looked back. Her mother was right behind her. But she wasn't normal. Something was wrong with her eyes.*

*They were no longer Mummy's eyes. They were red, and worse, they looked slanted, like the eyes of a wolf.*

*Her mother's smile turned into something bad, something wicked. She grabbed Emma's wrist and squeezed.*

*"Mummy, you're hurting me. Let go." She tried to yank back, to pull herself free, but couldn't. "Mummmeee!" she screamed, as Mummy's claw-like fingers tightened, pulling her toward her, back into the other room away from the stairs, away from Lucia.*

*And toward the wolves.*

Emma sat upright in bed, her heart pounding, her head throbbing. She grabbed her left wrist with her right hand and rubbed it and, for a second, she could still feel her mother's painful grasp. She wiped the tears off her cheeks. "Damn." She took three deep breaths, and tried to calm her racing heart. She hadn't had one of those dreams in so long, and now this would make three nights in a row.

She had to think of something else. Something good. Something happy. She couldn't go back to sleep thinking of her mother that way. She didn't want to have that dream again. *Think about Damien, Emma.* The voice whispered through her mind, bringing forth the image of piercing blue eyes and thoughts of the way he looked at her and the way his touch lingered.

She sat up and looked at Angel's empty bed under the window. In the past, whenever she'd had a nightmare, Angel would be there for her, licking her face, distracting her from the dream. But she wasn't here now. Worry filled her. She sat up in the bed, trying not to think of her mother, and trying not to think of Angel and where she might be.

Emma let herself think of Damien. She knew it was dangerous to think of him, knew it was the curse drawing her toward him, but she couldn't help wondering what it would feel like to lie in his arms. To have someone who cared about her there to chase the bad dreams away. She sighed.

She lay back down and closed her eyes, taking several deep breaths, and concentrated on relaxing—deep one in, long one out, deep one in, long one out. She pictured herself floating in a white cloud, surrounded by the warm light of the sun. Peace overcame her and she felt herself drifting.

And then she heard the soft whimper. She tensed, her eyes flying open. "Angel?"

She sat upright in bed, listening intently. There it was again, the soft mewling sound of a frightened animal. Her little dog was out there somewhere scared and alone. She shot out of bed and rushed to the door. Trying not to make a sound, she cracked it open, hoping Angel would be standing there waiting in the hall, but she was nowhere to be seen, and the whimpering sounds were growing fainter. Emma shut the door and hurried to the window.

In the faint glow from the outdoor lights, she saw a small white shape huddled in the middle of the maze. *Angel!* Fear slammed into her chest. She pulled on her robe and ran out of her room, down the stairs and into the kitchen toward the back door. She grabbed the knob and turned it just as the wolf stepped into her peripheral vision. She gasped and froze. They were all out there, all four of them, hovering close to the back door.

Waiting for her?

She heard the soft whimper again, and saw the wolves' ears prick and their heads turn toward the maze. "Damn!" How was she going to get out there? The large one got up and sauntered toward the maze. "Be quiet, Angel!"

She considered going out the front door and running around the long way, but knew it would take too long. Not to mention the three other wolves who could easily catch up with her. She looked down the hall toward Lucia's quarters and considered running for help. But she knew what Lucia would say. "Don't go. She'll be fine."

But would she? Could she take that chance? She knew it was beyond crazy, but she couldn't leave Angel out there all alone. With that…thing. She looked out the back door window again, trying to figure out what to do.

The large wolf was gone, already inside the maze. The other three looked at her. Waiting.

She turned and stared at the cellar door, now shut tight within the wall. Through that door, there was a passage from the cellar to the maze. Her stomach twisted into a tight knot. She had to go down there, she had to suck it up and face the dark, it was the only way.

Her stomach fluttered as she walked toward the door.

She hadn't been down there since that night so long ago, when her mother died and she was left alone with the wolves. She hovered near the door, and broke out in a cold sweat. She had no choice. If she didn't go down into that cellar and find her way out to the maze, her dog, the only true joy in her life, would be ripped to shreds. She couldn't let that happen.

She reached for the panel door and pushed on the upper right-hand corner. She stepped back as it sprung open. Her heart thumped louder than a bass drum as she stared down into the darkness. She placed her hand on the rail, but couldn't take the first step. Something within her screamed for her to stop, to find a different way. To forget the dog.

But she couldn't. Angel wasn't just any old dog. She'd been her constant companion, the one she'd shared her dreams and secrets with. She wouldn't abandon her. It will be fine, she told herself. There's nothing down there. No one waiting for her.

The scent she'd smelled earlier still lingered, and she now recognized it as one of Lucia's sticks of incense. That's all, just Lucia and her magic. Nothing to be worried about, she told herself.

She stepped into the darkness and onto the rickety wooden steps, then leaned forward and pulled the chain hanging from a bare bulb set in the ceiling. Dim light filled the room, but didn't extend far into the cellar's corners. She saw a flashlight waiting on the shelf at the bottom of the staircase and hurried to pick it up.

She glanced to her left toward the room from her

dreams. Had all that really happened? She wished she knew for sure, but she couldn't remember anything other than waking in the hospital and being told her mother was dead. Everyone had said they'd been attacked by a pack of rogue dogs.

But she knew better. There were no rogue dogs. Only wolves, always the wolves.

She turned away from the room and whatever might have happened there and followed the darkened pathway on the right, moving deeper beneath the house. It was better for her not to think about it too much. There was a reason her mind blocked out what had happened that night. The doctors had told her so. But still, part of her wondered if she could remember maybe the dreams would stop.

After a few moments, the passageway narrowed and the heavy scent of earth thickened, closing around her. She'd followed this path before, many times with her mother when she'd been young. She had nothing to be afraid of, she told herself. Nothing.

Unfortunately, the thoughts of wisdom didn't stop the fear from coiling in her belly and snaking around her heart. She walked slowly, listening intently, shining the dim light along the earthen and rock walls, and the heavy wooden beams that kept them in place. She wasn't sure how far she'd gone before she reached the end of the passageway.

She shone the light over six or seven iron bars bored horizontally into the earthen wall, forming a ladder. She moved the light up the ladder to the trapdoor above her.

It was small and obviously built many years ago. They had probably added this tunnel in here at the time the house was built as a way for the family to escape during a crisis.

There was so much she didn't know about her family history, she thought, as she climbed up the ladder. At the top, she reached up and pulled on the rusty bolt that held the trapdoor in place. The bolt protested and groaned under her touch before finally sliding back.

She pushed upward on the wooden door. It opened, falling backward beyond her reach into a small enclosure. She climbed up into a cramped round space. And then she remembered. She was inside the cherub's fountain in the middle of the maze. She pulled back another latch, and a door in the base of the statue opened. She crawled out into the center of the maze, and heard a soft whimper.

"Angel," she whispered, and heard a rustling to her right. She moved around the fountain, and saw her dog crouching beneath a hedge, shivering in the moonlight. Relief overwhelmed her, causing a lump to lodge in her throat.

Quickly, she crawled toward her dog, scooped it out of the hedge and nestled it against her chest. "What are you doing out here?" she cooed, snuggling the dog against her. Angel's little tail thumped against her chest as her tongue washed across her face.

"All right," Emma said, and couldn't help the wide grin as she pulled back from the sneaky little tongue. "You're all right," she assured the dog, and herself, as she quickly ran her hand over the dog's body, searching for any bumps or lesions. Before she could finish her assessment and crawl back into the fountain, a wolf rounded a corner and stepped onto the path in front of her. Emma clutched Angel tighter.

The wolf stared at her, its eyes flashing red. In sheer terror, Emma edged backward toward the statue. The wolf started to move, slowly, creeping toward her.

"What do you want?" she whispered, hoping the sound of her voice would stop the animal. But it didn't.

Her heart pounded and her breath ached in her chest, but she forced herself to move slowly, inching away from the beast, when what she really wanted to do was jump up and run, then take a headlong dive into the statue. But she knew she couldn't. Not only was the animal faster than her, the opening in the fountain's base was too small, too awkward.

Steadily, she made her way backward, never taking her eyes off the beast, until her feet brushed against the marble base. She crouched down, lowering herself onto her belly, knowing she was making herself even more vulnerable, as she pushed backward into the cramped statue.

The wolf approached her, and leaned in. His wide jaw opened, and she could smell the hot, foul odor of his breath. She cringed, trying to draw back. Why was it just staring at her? Why not attack? Angel whimpered, and stiffened in her grasp, trying to scurry away from the wolf.

Emma continued edging backward, and when her

legs were all the way in the statue and dangling down the trapdoor, she shoved herself through, landing hard on the ground in the bottom of the passageway. She dropped Angel, then scrambled up the ladder to secure the trapdoor. The wolf's head was in the base of the fountain, looking in at her. She grabbed the trapdoor, and pulled it closed, then tried to secure the bolt into place, but it caught. Finally, the tip slid into the socket and held.

She blew out a huge sigh of relief, then dropped back down to the ground. She sat there for a moment, staring up at the door waiting to make sure there was no way the wolf could open it, then, once her heart slowed to a somewhat normal rhythm, she picked up Angel and the flashlight and headed back toward the kitchen.

## Chapter 5

"I heard you tell Emma you're staying the night," Lucia said to Damien, as if she didn't quite believe he would.

"I think that would be best, don't you?" Damien walked toward the windows as he heard the wolves dashing away from the house. He peered out and saw them racing away, and couldn't help wondering what had captured their interest.

"I really don't see how you think your presence here will help. Emma's already asleep, why don't you come back tomorrow?" Lucia suggested with a slight narrowing of her eyes. "We will do better without the Cadre in this house."

"Miss McGovern asked me to stay," Damien said absently. He listened intently, reaching with his vampire senses. His brother Nicholai and the others like him were out there. Not too far away.

"Emma was just being polite," Lucia responded. "Too polite for her own good, if you ask me."

"You really think you can do better on your own?" he asked, growing annoyed with the woman's meddling.

"I've managed all these years."

He turned and faced her. "But you couldn't save her mother. What makes you think you can save Emma?"

A sliver of pain flashed through Lucia's eyes, and then it was gone. "We would have been fine, if the Cadre agent hadn't come. He set the Curse in motion. He and Audrey, they—" She shook her head and closed her eyes, the bitter regret clear on her face. "If it hadn't been for the Cadre's meddling, Emma's mother would be alive today."

Damien could see her point. "How exactly did the agent die?" he asked.

"Audrey killed him. Even though she loved him, she couldn't help herself. The Curse was stronger than they were."

"And Emma's father?" Damien gestured for her to go ahead of him, wanting her to move farther into the house. He wanted to see out back. Something was out there. He could hear the wolves scurrying, and could sense the vampire presence growing stronger.

"Audrey never loved him," Lucia said in a hushed

voice and pointed toward the ceiling as she continued down the hall. "Now, don't get me wrong, she cared for him, but it was more of an arrangement, as had been most of the marriages in this family. The ones that weren't—" she shook her head as sadness filled her face "—they didn't end well."

"Oh," he muttered, but he wasn't really listening. Instead he was focused on the vampires outside. They were close, he could feel their need, their hunger.

"So, you see," Lucia said as she walked into the kitchen, "Audrey and Mr. McGovern could have continued on here at Wolvesrain with no one to bother them, no one to interfere in their lives, and the Curse could have been forgotten—if the Cadre hadn't interfered."

Damien leaned back against the wall. "And Emma wouldn't have been attacked by wolves. She would have grown up well-adjusted and loved, she would have wanted to go to university, to have friends, to have a normal life. She would have wanted to find love."

"You think she doesn't want love now? I hear her crying at night, but she's been warned."

"As her mother was?"

Lucia turned away, but as she did, the implication of her words sat heavy in his mind. A family doomed to a life without love. An old familiar ache twisted his heart. Had his life been much different? Sometimes life without love, without the complications of emotions, was infinitely better.

He crossed the kitchen and peered out the window.

His gaze rested on the family cemetery perched on a hillside, protected by an overgrown thicket of briars and enclosed by a rusted iron fence. A marble angel sat in the center, her beautiful chin lifted skyward, her wings chipped and darkened with age.

In the deepening shadows stretching across weathered granite tombs and gnarled oaks, figures moved quicker than the human eye could follow, jumping stealthily among the gravestones in a macabre dance of perverse glee.

Lucia took off her apron and hung it on the back of the pantry door. "I suppose what's done is done. You're here, nothing to be done about that. Saving Emma is what matters now."

"That's why the Cadre sent me," he muttered.

She looked skeptical, but he saw a flicker of hope enter her eyes.

She turned toward the stairs, but as she did, a portion of the wall behind her opened, and Emma stepped into the kitchen in a dusty robe. Cobwebs danced in her hair and dirt smudged her chin, and she was clutching a small dirty dog tight to her chest. Her eyes widened and she gasped as she saw them and the dog immediately started barking.

"Good Lord in heaven," Lucia said, and brought a trembling hand to her chest. "You just about stopped my heart. What were you doing down there?"

"Sorry," Emma said, and rushed past them. "Angel was locked in the cellar."

Disbelief crossed Lucia's face as she watched Emma run up the stairs, but she didn't say anything.

Damien watched Emma disappear around the bend above them, and wondered what she'd been up to. He glanced at the panel door, sitting slightly open from the wall. Whatever it was, Lucia hadn't believed it was to retrieve the dog.

He followed the housekeeper up to the second floor. He'd give her a few moments to get back downstairs before heading out to find Nicholai and discover what he could about this vampire clan Nica had spoken of. Now that the Cadre knew they were here, it was only a matter of time before they sent a crew out after them.

He couldn't let Nicholai be trapped by the Cadre. No matter that they hadn't spoken since he'd been reborn, he wouldn't wish the Cadre's way of dealing with vampires on any of his kind.

And certainly not on his brother.

Lucia led him down a long corridor decorated with gold silk wallpaper patterned with tiny fleur de lis above dark paneled wainscoting three-quarters of the way up the wall. She paused a moment outside a closed door, leaning in close to listen. He reached with his senses, and felt Emma inside, murmuring to her dog. He stifled a smile. If you could call the little rat a dog.

After a second, Lucia continued forward to the last room on the right. She opened the door and stepped inside. "Will this do?"

He walked in behind her, noticing the heavy draperies that matched the gold brocade bedspread. A large armoire sat against the wall next to the window. He could easily slide that over the window and block out most of the sun's damaging light.

He wasn't as sensitive to the sun's rays as he had once been, and was frequently tempted to take the chance and see how much his skin could stand. Was he old enough now? Or would he burst into flames as he'd seen happen to the fledglings who couldn't find shelter? What he wouldn't give to spend just an hour out in the blessed light, and discover if his memory of the warmth against his skin was accurate, or if perhaps he was just a man who desired that which he couldn't have. Hope, sunshine, love—the sweet optimism that humans take for granted that everything in life has a purpose, and goodness will always prevail.

"Yes, it will be fine," he answered. "It is only for one day. Emma and I will leave for St. Yve tomorrow evening."

Lucia's lips twisted with disapproval. She stared at him for a moment, as if there was something more she wanted to say, but then nodded and left without saying another word. Thankful, he shut the door behind her and waited, listening until he could no longer hear her footsteps. After he was certain she was gone, he returned to the back staircase and down into the kitchen, quickly moving toward the back door.

Emma took in her appearance in the full-length mirror in the corner. She still felt the flush of embarrassment seeping through her. She hadn't expected to see anyone in the kitchen, certainly not Damien.

And she in her robe with dirt on her face! She could just sink into the floor and die. She took off the robe, and climbed into a hot shower. She washed all the dirt and cobwebs off her, all the while thinking of Damien. She'd never met a man like him before, not that she'd had a lot of exposure to men, but the ones she had met never had that sense of power about them.

He carried an aura of strength about him, as if he could do anything. He hadn't even flinched when he'd seen the wolves. She was drawn to him in ways she'd never felt before, ways she only hoped she'd be able to hide. Why would a man like him, with such confidence and worldliness, ever find anything interesting about a woman like her? A woman who had spent her whole life holed up in a crumbling castle?

She turned off the shower, toweled off and got back into bed. She took a long look at Angel curled up on her pillow under the window, and hoped that little dogs wouldn't always be her only companions.

She nestled deep under the covers and tried not to think of Damien right down the hall. But she couldn't help it. Was he really as open to her thoughts and feelings as he appeared? Was there any chance he was thinking of her, too?

Stop it! she told herself. She was being ridiculous, acting like a silly schoolgirl. She put him out of her mind and focused on the candle flame flickering next to her bed. Her heartbeat slowed and her breathing evened as her mind drifted back to Damien.

A soft touch moved across her skin. She sighed as the

whispered sensations ran freely over her naked body, warming her, making her skin jump and tingle. She felt a slight pressure on her mouth and smiled. He was kissing her, his tongue slipping between her lips.

His touch was sweet, almost tentative. His caress moved to her cheek and down her throat, stopping on her breast, leaving chills in its wake. He kissed her again, stroking her sensitive skin as their lips met, his touch growing firmer, more demanding, as the heat built within her.

He pinched her nipples, playfully plucking the hardened nubs. She sighed and arched into him, wanting more, wanting the pleasure moving through her body to continue. She was dreaming, yes? She had to be, and yet, it felt so real. It felt so good.

He kissed her again, deep and insistent. She reached up and entwined her fingers in the tangles of his long dark hair. A lingering touch moved to the inside of her thighs. She twisted, loving the delicious sensations moving through her. He smoothed and stroked her hair, probing her most private areas, and bringing a sweet gasp from her lips.

A large pressure pushed against her, and then it was inside her, velvety and huge. She sighed and then shuddered as it filled the expanse of her, stroking, slow at first, then faster. She reveled in the crush of his weight. Heat swelled within her with the pulsing between her legs. The pressure heightened, surging through her. She bunched the sheets in her fists and arched her back, trying to get closer. Wanting it deeper.

A light sheen of perspiration covered her skin as he touched that special place within her, making her scream out loud. Again and again, he drove into her until her breath caught, and her body shook with shudders that curled her toes.

On a choking pleasure-filled gasp her eyes flew open. No one was with her.

Damien stepped out of the kitchen and followed a gravel path along the back of the house until he reached the edge of what had once been an intricate English garden, but had now fallen to neglect and decay. He passed by an overgrown and misshapen maze, then continued until he reached the forest.

Over the years, he'd met other vampires, had even been welcomed into their clans, but he found their excesses morbid and self-indulgent. They had no curiosity about their origins, and no purpose other than to feed and frolic. He knew better, but still found himself hoping this group would be different. As soon as he finished this last job for the Cadre, he'd like to find some place where he belonged; he'd like to believe that what he'd heard about his brother wasn't true. He'd like to reconnect with Nicholai.

The sound was faint at first, but as he focused on it, it became stronger, filling his mind. Whispering. Laughing. Voices—male, female. And with the sounds of their romping, he could hear something else, something more—Emma McGovern's name slipping off their tongues.

Worry tightened his chest. Then the smell of blood—
thick, rich, and aromatic—reached him and twisted in
his gut. The taste filled his mouth. He closed his eyes,
as the sharp pain of need almost doubled him over.

He'd found the vampires.

Laughter, music and revelry sounded in the distance.
He moved quicker and, as he got closer, the sounds intensified. The faint glow of a fire shone through the
bushes, smoke filled the air. He kept to the outskirts of
the camp, moving quickly.

He took a deep breath, and focused on clearing his
mind to shield himself from them, but more to protect
himself from the need burning within him. The need
for blood.

He focused inward, envisioning fields of heather
wafting in the breeze, the warmth of the sun's rays on his
face. Mentally he surrounded himself in a purple cloud.
He was stronger than the hunger. He was invisible to the
vampire's radar. A feeling of calm dropped over him, and
he knew he was back in control.

He moved silently, keeping his mental shields in
place. No reason to make his presence known until he
knew exactly who and what he was dealing with. Until
he knew for certain what kind of vampire his brother
had become. If he had, in fact, been tainted by feeding
off demon essence.

He stood behind a tree and watched three gypsy
women in long, flowing, brightly colored skirts dance
around the fire in the center of the clearing. As they
stamped their feet, long strips of bangles attached to

skimpy tops clinked and jingled in melodic symphony. Their arms moved in fluid motion about their heads and out to the sides, an invitation to love. Two men accompanied them on guitars, their music lively, the dance enthralling.

He hadn't seen a true gypsy dance in years. He stood, watching, mesmerized. As the smell of incense filled the air, drifting on the cool breeze, he could easily imagine it was 1761 again, and Camilla was one of those women using her charms to captivate the Englishmen into losing their hearts and emptying their pockets.

"Damien."

The familiar voice filled his mind, an instant before the tickle of breath heated the back of his neck. He spun round. Nicholai stood before him, his eyes eerily reflecting the fire's light, a wicked smile playing across his face—a face that looked very much as it had the last time he'd seen him, in this very forest more than two hundred years ago.

"Hello, brother," Nicholai said.

Damien tried to speak, but something caught in his throat, some emotion from long ago. His pleasure must have shone in his eyes, for Nicholai opened his arms and stepped forward, and the two men embraced.

"I had always wondered what it would be like to see you again," Damien muttered.

Nicholai laughed.

"Where have you been?" Damien asked. "All this time. I've heard rumors but never knew for sure."

"I could ask the same of you, dear brother. But then

I already know. Everyone knows of Damien, the demon hunter. Your reputation precedes you."

"Does it?" Damien asked, at once put on guard by the tone of his brother's voice. He remembered that tone from Nicholai's propensity to throw down a challenge.

"So, are you here to hunt Asmos this time?" Nicholai pressed.

Damien stiffened. He knew Nicholai and his clan were after the demon's essence, had remembered Emma's name drifting off their lips. His hope for a warm reunion dissipated like an aged balloon slowly being crushed beneath the weight of reality. "Does it matter?" he asked.

"I wouldn't be here if it didn't."

"You were expecting me then?" Damien pressed.

"I was hoping." Nicholai smiled, a warm, brotherly smile, except for the chill buried deep within his eyes.

"It's good to see you, Nicholai," Damien said, offering the proverbial olive branch and hoping for the best. "I'd heard rumors myself, but did not know for certain…."

"No, you wouldn't. Our parents stole you away, their precious son, riding deep into the night and taking you to the secret castle in the south."

"You know of St. Yve?" Damien asked, though he wasn't surprised.

"We've heard of it, and have searched many times, but to no avail. Other than running into some nasty faeries in the forest surrounding, we have never come close. Perhaps you will show us the way? Give us a tour of your new home."

"Why?" Damien asked, again on guard, wondering why his brother would be so interested in an old order that hunts the supernatural. Wondering if Nicholai had any idea what would have happened to him had he gotten anywhere near St. Yve.

"The secrets of time and space lie buried within those walls, dear brother. That and so much more."

Damien thought of the vampires imprisoned beneath and within the castle walls, and the thousands of demons captured within the crystals throughout the centuries. Nicholai, like their maker, fed off demon essence. From what Damien understood, it worked to make them more powerful, but it twisted their minds, giving them a brutal, ruthless edge.

St. Yve had an entire dungeon filled with demon-containment crystals. A veritable demon-essence smorgasbord for the likes of vampires like his brother. "Really, never saw anything like that in the couple of hundred or so years that I lived there," Damien replied.

"Perhaps you didn't look hard enough," Nicholai challenged. "But now that you're here, we can visit St. Yve together." He clapped him on the back. "Come, meet everyone."

Damien chilled. Would Nicholai try and force him into taking him to St. Yve? He shuddered at the thought, at what would happen to them all. He followed his brother into the clearing, quickly taking inventory of the number of vampires, counting an even twelve.

He could hear their whispers, his brethren, plotting their madness to obtain the demon essence. A shudder moved through him. He was strong and older than most of the vampires there, but did the essence running through their veins give them an advantage? Would their sheer numbers make him fair game?

The dancing and music stopped as soon as he and Nicholai walked into the clearing. The vampires stared at him, some with open curiosity, others with obvious hostility. "Everyone, come meet my long-lost brother, Damien," Nicholai invited.

Damien stood very still as the vampires circled around him. There were seven men, wary and suspicious, who took his measure, while the five women, obviously intrigued, smiled and touched him. A couple rubbed themselves provocatively against him, promising...everything. He smiled at them, while reaching with his mind to try and get a sense of the emotions of the group.

"Enjoy yourself, brother," Nicholai said. "We mean you no harm."

A vampire with long black hair and incredible dark eyes slipped her hand beneath his shirt, softly stroking his chest, running her fingers down his ribcage, over the soft leather of his pants. His cock responded, and her red-painted lips stretched into a lustful smile.

Nicholai grabbed a redhead by the wrist and yanked her to him. He dragged his nail along the vein in her neck, slicing open the skin. He suckled it, drinking the sweet drink, and her eyelids fluttered and closed, her mouth opening on a moan.

Damien knew vampires fed off one another as an

erotic act, but it wasn't one he'd ever tried. Though, he must admit to being curious, to wanting. He licked his lips and turned back to the brunette.

"Stick around," Nicholai said. "We have much to discuss."

Damien looked at the temptress offering herself to him, and fiercely wanted to pull her to him, to feel her soft womanly curves against him, to bury his face between her ample breasts. "I can't stay long," he said, even as his breathing quickened.

Nicholai laughed, and continued his ministrations on the redhead, who was obviously enjoying his feeding off her very much. The desire to give the same pleasure to the woman standing before Damien was almost overpowering.

The woman dropped to her knees in front of him, her hand on the buttons that loosened his pants. She looked up at him, her eyes meeting his, and a sudden whirl of impressions filled him—hunger, deceit, death. *Madness.*

Damien put a hand on hers stopping her. "I need to go," he said, his voice cracking.

"That's right," Nicholai said. "You need to run back to Wolvesrain and protect the next vessel. Why bother, little brother? It's her destiny."

Damien stared at him, suddenly certain that he'd stepped into a trap. Through him they wanted to breach Wolvesrain, they wanted Emma. The woman pulled at his pants again. Damien pushed her away and stepped back.

His brother smiled and lapped again at the

redhead's neck. Damien reached with his mind, searching for his brother's true intentions, but hit a wall. He couldn't read him.

"Try as you might, you're not as powerful as I, little brother."

"Aren't I?" Damien asked. "We aren't children anymore."

"No, but you deny yourself the human elixir you need to make yourself strong." He took a long lick. "The blood will set you free."

"In that denial, I am stronger."

Nicholai laughed. "You deny who you are. What you are. As a vampire, you are a strong, powerful predator with the compassion and intelligence to determine when to spare life and when to deliver death."

In the time it took Damien to draw in a breath, his brother kicked Damien's legs out from under him. He hit the ground, lying flat on his back with Nicholai's boot planted square on his chest.

"Who's the strongest?" Nicholai mocked.

Damien's stomach clenched. His fists squeezed into tight balls of rage. Ever since they were children his brother had delighted in this game. He grabbed Nicholai's boot in both hands and twisted, knocking his brother to the ground, where he rolled on top of him, pinning him flat. "I am."

His brother laughed out loud. "We'll see about that, won't we?" With a burst of speed, Nicholai had Damien on his back. "You too can have the strength of the gods, Damien. It's right there in front of you, pulsing through

Miss McGovern's beautiful neck." He leaned down and kissed Damien on the cheek. "All you have to do is take a bite," he whispered, then he was gone.

Stunned, Damien sat up and rubbed his brother's kiss off his face. He searched the area around him with his mind, reaching for his brother's presence, but couldn't find him. Either his brother was gone using speed Damien had never seen, or he was masking himself. A feat Damien hadn't been able to manage, since Nicholai seemed to have sensed him, easily.

What Damien had feared was true: Nicholai's strength was beyond his. And if Nicholai went after Emma? Would he wait to see if the curse was fulfilled and she became Asmos's vessel? Or would he just go after the essence she already had in her now, thanks to the demon wolves? Either way wasn't good. Damien got up and, moving as fast as he could, left the clearing and the gypsy vampire clan behind. He had to get Emma out of Wolvesrain and to the safety of St. Yve. Tonight!

## Chapter 6

The wolves loped through the woods, their hunger surging through them, heating their blood and switching their senses to full alert. They circled the graveyard, catching the scent of others like themselves; others filled with the essence of the Dark Realm. The moon rose higher in the sky urging them forward, as did the voice of their master, whispering in their minds.

In the distance, they could see the manor rising above the fog. The lights in the windows looked different than they had in years past. A steady glow shone through the hard glass, instead of the flickering that matched their racing heartbeats.

As a group, they raced toward the maze, the hard

earth giving way beneath their paws. The girl lay in the house, the one their master claimed. They could smell her, could feel her waiting for them, could remember the taste of her blood.

They stopped outside the maze, aware of the vampires close by. First one, then the others lifted their heads and let loose a slight moan, rising in pitch as they stared up at the moon and emptied the pent-up fervor in their chests, letting it spew forth in a hair-raising howl that sent rabbits and deer alike scampering for safety.

Ignoring the vampires, they entered the maze, finding their way to the center as they had many times before. The door at the base of the fountain opened easily to their practiced touch, and so did the bolt in the door below, after they shimmied the door back and forth. They jumped down beneath the ground, through the passage and into the cellar.

Moving quietly, they rushed up through the panel door and into the kitchen and up the back staircase. The night of the Equinox was almost upon them. Soon their master would be free.

Damien ran so fast, he practically flew through the woods. He had to get back to Wolvesrain. One way or another, Nicholai was going to go after Emma, and Damien wasn't sure if he was strong enough to stop him. As he approached the house, he stopped at his Mercedes, opened the trunk, and pulled out his silver dagger and two iron-cored ash-wood stakes.

Even before he closed the trunk, he heard the soft tread of footsteps moving quickly toward the house. Damien reached out with his mind, searching for his brother's presence, and sensed him nearby. Closer than he should be.

He pulled on his long black leather coat and pocketed the weapons. He hurried up the front steps and rang the bell, then waited impatiently for Lucia to answer. He could have just walked in, but he didn't want to freak the woman out any more than she already seemed to be. He could hear her trudging down the hall, a lot slower than he'd have liked.

Finally the door opened. Her eyes widened in surprise as she looked at him. "I thought you were upstairs in bed?"

"I decided to take a walk. You mind?"

"Do I have a choice?" she asked, with a slight crinkling of her nose, as if she smelled something bad, but he doubted she could smell anything over the stench of the garlic she wore around her neck.

He took a step back, and waited for her to step aside. She didn't. "May I come in?" he asked.

"I've already invited you once. Do we need to stand on formalities?"

"Thank you," he said and tipped his head forward in a slight bow. Out of the corner of his eye, he saw movement coming out of the line of trees at the edge of the forest.

She moved back, allowing him to pass then shut the door firmly behind him.

"So, is that for me?" he asked, pointing toward her newly-fashioned garlic and wolfsbane necklace.

She looked at him surreptitiously. "It doesn't affect you?"

He shrugged. "Stinks something fierce. You don't have to worry about me giving you a kiss."

She narrowed her eyes and almost said something, but must have thought better of it, for her lips tightened into a thin line. She took off the necklace and hung it on the doorknob. Other than the smell, garlic didn't bother him, but he hated wolfsbane. It made him itchy.

"Just to be safe, do me a favor and don't invite anyone else in tonight," he said, casually.

"As if I would," she muttered.

Damien almost grinned. In an odd way, she reminded him of his aunt Trudy, fiercely protective to the point of rudeness. Since he didn't think she'd be shocked, he decided to be blunt. "You should know there are vampires surrounding the house. I've decided it would be safest to take Emma to St. Yve tonight. Will you and Mr. McGovern be all right here alone?"

She opened up a special door under the stairs and took out a silver dagger and a box of pencil-thin stakes, which she laid on the table next to a crossbow. "Any doubts?"

Damien was just about to comment, when he heard the soft footfalls of wolves' feet. He stilled, listening intently, trying to pinpoint their location. The scent of brimstone wafted down from the second floor. "Emma!"

"What is it?" Lucia asked, and grabbed up the dagger.

"The wolves," he said, and bolted for the stairs, taking them two at a time. Why hadn't he noticed the wolves weren't outside when he returned? They were always hovering, and yet they weren't there.

He ran down the hall, as Emma's screams pierced the house. Images of Emma trying to fight off the beasts assaulted his mind. At the end of the hall, her bedroom door gaped open. Flickering candlelight bounced and shimmered off the wooden floor.

He hesitated as he reached her door, her sudden silence worrying him more than her screams. He steeled himself for what he might find, and stepped into her room.

Emma was sitting up in her bed, her hands clutching the blankets to her, as she stared in shocked horror at the wolves on either side of her. They stood as he walked through the door and turned toward him, growling low in their throats and baring their sharp fangs. For a second, he considered showing them his own, but thought better of it as he turned to Emma.

"They won't touch you," Damien said softly, and walked slowly into the room. "See, they're sitting outside the protection circle. They won't cross it." He eased toward the animals, keeping his eye on the closest one as it lifted its snout into a vicious snarl. He grabbed the silver dagger out of his pocket and slowly approached.

"Back away," Lucia said as she hurried through the door behind him. She carried a piece of burning fabric raised high in front of her. A noxious smell filled the room. Nausea cramped Damien's stomach, and he doubled in two. The wolves whined, then ran past them out of the room.

Grabbing her robe around her, and clutching the little dog that had been cowering under the covers, Emma jumped out of the bed and ran toward Lucia. The older woman dropped the burning rag into the sink, then turned and gave Emma a big hug.

"Thank God," Lucia murmured.

"I don't understand," Emma asked. "They've never come in the house before. How'd they get in?"

"I don't know, but I'll find out." Damien followed the wolves' descent through the house. If they could get in, so could Nicholai and his vamps. Two more wolves raced passed him, these coming from another room behind him. Concerned, Damien glanced down the hall, wondering where they'd been, and what they'd been up to.

He followed the wolves down the back staircase that led to the kitchen, then continued through the opened cellar door, the one Emma had come through earlier clutching her dog. Moving cautiously, he approached the door and pulled it all the way open, then stared down into a dimly lit cellar.

The bulb still burned, but didn't extend far enough into the corners to betray whether the wolves might be lying in wait. He reached with his senses, focusing on the space around him, searching for a presence beneath the house. He was alone.

He hurried down the stairs and followed a dank corridor under the house until the passageway narrowed and the heady scent of earth thickened, closing around him. He stopped abruptly as he reached the end of the passageway.

In near darkness, he felt around him, his hand brushing against the earth-and-rock walls and the heavy wooden beams above him. A whisper of night air touched his cheek, and filled his nose. He looked up and saw the soft glow of moonlight through a small rectangular opening.

A trapdoor. He listened for a moment to make sure the wolves had left and no one else was there, then reached up, pulled the door closed and struggled to slide the heavy metal bolt into place. He pushed against the door, making sure it would stay closed. How did the wolves know it was there? Did Nicholai?

Anxiety twisted through him, as he frowned in the darkness. A faint scream filled the tunnels. His breath caught. He turned and ran toward Emma's gut-wrenching moans.

As he reached the storage room under the kitchen, the crying stopped, and the house suddenly grew silent. He paused at the bottom of the stairs, reaching out with his mind for Nicholai's presence, or that of his bloodthirsty cohorts, but felt nothing. Nor were the wolves back.

Unable to determine the threat, he hurried up into the kitchen, then up to the second floor. Lucia was in the hall, a look of despair on her face. "It's Mr. McGovern," she said, quietly.

Damien stepped past her into the room. Emma was lying on her father's bed, her shoulders trembling with grief as she wept quietly next to her father's still body. His skin was grayish and clammy, his chest barely moving as the man struggled to breathe.

Damien sighed and started to reach for Emma, wanting to touch her, to offer some comfort, but he hesitated. From what he knew of Mr. McGovern, he had a weak heart. He didn't know how he could help. And worse, he didn't know how he'd be able to get her to leave him.

He started to turn away to leave her alone, when he noticed the muddy paw prints on the coverlet, and on the carpet at his feet.

*The wolves.*

This was where they had been, but what had they been up to? He walked around the far side of the bed, away from Emma and took a good look at the man. A wicked-looking scratch or bite marred his shoulder. "We should get him to St. Yve."

Emma looked up at him, her eyes swollen with tears. "Why? What can they do?"

"Hopefully, help. But if they're going to, we'll have to get him there right away. Can you leave now?"

She nodded, and ran out of the room. As she did, Damien scooped her father up off the bed, easily cradling the fragile man in his arms. Lucia gave him a look full of skepticism. "I'm telling the truth," he offered, though he wasn't sure why he bothered. The old woman nodded and followed him down the hall. It only took Emma a minute, and she was rushing down the stairs after him, a small bag in her hand.

"Be careful," Lucia called from the top of the stairs. She bent down and lifted Angel into her arms.

"Remember what I said. Let no one in," Damien warned.

She nodded, her face looking grave. Damien turned back to Emma as they hurried through the house. "If we leave now, we can easily make St. Yve before morning."

"And they'll know what to do to help my father?"

"If the wolves have caused him any harm, they should be able to counteract the damage." Damien hesitated as they reached the front door. The strand of garlic and wolfsbane was still wrapped around the knob, blocking his ability to sense if Nicholai was waiting on the other side of the door. He shifted the old man in his arms.

"I've got it," Emma said, and reached around him for the door, pulling it open before Damien could warn her against it.

He sucked in a breath, one hand grabbing the door in case he needed to slam it shut, but all looked clear. No sign of Nicholai and his gang anywhere in sight. Obviously, a ruse. "Keep the necklace with you," he said on a rushed breath, knowing it would cause a great deal of distress to many of Nicholai's fledglings if they came into contact with it. He took the lead as he hurried out the door and toward the car.

Emma grimaced as she placed the wolfsbane and

garlic around her neck. She ran ahead of him, pulling open the door, then stepped back as Damien placed her father in the small backseat.

"Get in," he ordered, and ran toward the driver's side. Now that he could no longer smell the garlic, he could sense the vampires close by. Too close. Before he could reach the driver's door, the red-haired vampire who'd been with his brother stepped out from behind a tree, blocking his path, a wicked smile on her face. "Going somewhere?"

He stopped, and stiffened his stance, legs apart, as he rolled up on the balls of his feet. "Back off and you won't get hurt," he warned.

She laughed. A tall man he hadn't recalled seeing before stepped out from behind the car. "Give us the girl, and you can leave. Then no one will get hurt."

"Somehow I'm not feeling the love here," Damien said, and cocked a wicked smile of his own.

The vampire jutted up his chin in response, gesturing toward Emma. Another vampire with short spiky hair opened Emma's door and gestured for her to get out of the car.

"Don't move, Emma," Damien said loudly, reaching with his mind, sensing more vamps descending on them from the other side of the house. Time was just about up.

The redhead and her thug took a step toward him. "Come on, darling. Give us the girl. We'll share."

From fifty yards off, Nicholai was quickly approaching with five or six of his vampires in tow. Damien could feel his brother reaching with his vampire senses, probing into Damien's mind, the pressure expanding as Nicholai tried to force his will upon him, a feat Damien had heard of, but had yet to accomplish himself. Perhaps Nicholai's powers of persuasion worked on others, but they weren't working this time.

Damien slipped his hands in the pockets of his leather jacket and grasped a stake in each fist. "Your lover is coming," Damien said. The vixen looked past him toward Nicholai. Damien advanced. In one fluid movement, he shoved the stake in his right hand deep into the woman's chest, then pivoted, and drove the other into the man. They both howled, the sound high-pitched and excruciating before they imploded, evaporating in clouds of dust.

A roar of pain and outrage filled the night air. Damien turned toward the raucous sound and saw Nicholai in the distance, his arms raised to the heavens, the sound erupting from his chest. The vampires around him fell back, shaken and confused. An avalanche of venomous anger struck Damien square in the chest, pushing him up against his car.

Emma screamed, adding to the cacophony of torment. The vampire with the spiky hair grabbed on to her arm and yanked her out of the car and up against him. Then, just as quickly, pushed her away from him, as the garlic and wolfsbane brushed up against his skin.

Damien braced one hand on the hood and catapulted himself over the car, extending both feet around and planting them in the vampire's chest, knocking him to the ground. He hurled himself on top of him and thrust a stake deep into his heart. The vampire obliterated beneath him into a pile of dust.

Damien stood, wiping the dust off his pants and saw Nicholai and his cohorts practically flying through the air toward them. He turned to Emma who was staring at him and the pile of dust at his feet in wide-eyed shock. Her head shot up as Nicholai's hate-filled roar filled the air.

"Quick, into the car," Damien ordered, and hurried toward the driver's seat. Emma's door barely closed as the engine roared to life. Damien dropped the Mercedes into gear as Nicholai threw himself against the car with a jarring thud. Emma screamed as they sped down the gravel drive. Losing his grip, Nicholai bounced off the car, hit the ground and rolled.

"Lucia!" Emma cried, as she looked out the window behind them. The old gypsy's outline was silhouetted in a top-floor window as she watched their escape.

"Don't worry. She'll be okay. She has weapons. She knows how to protect herself." He turned and looked at her. "Do me a favor and throw that necklace out the window."

Emma looked at him, did what he asked, then with a trembling voice asked, "Who were those… people?"

Damien watched his brother in the rearview mirror as he banded together with more and more of his clan. He remembered the strength of his brother's rage catapulting him against the car from fifty yards away, rage Nicholai had been able to control and use as a weapon. Damien had

never seen anything like that, had never felt anything like
it and, for an agonizing moment, he wondered how he
would be able to fight a force that powerful.

## Chapter 7

The moon's glow, the only light in a midnight sky on the lonely two-lane country road, became a beacon of normalcy in a world turned suddenly on end. A cold numbness stole over Emma, and she couldn't think, couldn't begin to comprehend what had happened back at Wolvesrain. She clutched herself and hunkered down in the passenger's seat.

There were so many things she wanted to say, to ask, but she couldn't seem to form the words. With a mounting roar, the Mercedes picked up speed, accelerating down the road, the smooth suspension hugging the turns. Intent on the road before him, Damien never hesitated, never slowed, hastening them forward as if the devil himself were on their tail.

And perhaps he was.

After what Emma had seen back at the house—and she still didn't know exactly what it was that she'd seen—she was no longer sure of anything. That man who'd grabbed her…he'd just disappeared. Damien had shoved something into his chest and—poof! Gone. Dust. Not for the first time since they'd left, shivers stole over her, threatening to shake loose what was left of her sanity.

"How're you holding up?" Damien asked and turned to look at her, the incandescent glow from the dashboard light casting shadows along his cheekbones and honing his jawline to a razor-sharp edge. She stilled, staring at the otherworldly sheen in his luminous eyes.

"Emma?"

The sound of her name emitting from his lips sent a quick thump to her already unsteady heartbeat.

"I don't know," she blurted. What could she say? That she was wondering if her tenuous grasp on reality had finally slipped?

He reached over and touched her arm. "It's okay. For tonight, the worst is over."

She wished she could believe him. Wished she could trust that things couldn't possibly get any worse. Unfortunately, she knew only too well that they could. She turned to glance at her father, lying on the backseat. His face was ghostly pale, but his breathing appeared to be steady.

If only he'd wake up and smile at her, and assure her

that everything would be all right, then maybe she could stop the trembling in her hands. But he looked so frail, so vulnerable, and she worried he might never wake.

"The Cadre has some of the best doctors in the country working with them," Damien said. "If something can be done to save him, they'll find it."

His words gave her hope. She took a deep breath and turned around to face the front, forcing back the tears that threatened to consume her. She would not cry. Not now. Not while there was still a chance that he was right, and something could be done.

"Why don't you try and get some rest? We won't be at St. Yve for a couple more hours."

Rest. The thought tempted her, and she wished she could, but fear and doubt kept racing around her mind. What was going to happen to them? And how could she place all her faith, her hope in the Cadre? Hadn't Lucia told her time and again that if it hadn't been for the Cadre, her mother would be alive and with them today? Any yet here she was, speeding down the road with a virtual stranger, being asked to put her father's life and her safety in their custody.

Her gaze once more fell to Damien's hands as they clutched the steering wheel. They weren't overly large hands. He wasn't an overly large man. There wasn't anything about him that was threatening, and yet she wasn't sure she could trust him. One minute he had her burning with desire and the next, she was quaking with utter fear.

"What happened back there?" she blurted, not

wanting to follow the direction her thoughts were taking, not sure she wanted to analyze them too much.

He hesitated, and she could tell he was debating whether or not to tell her.

"Please," she added. "That was my home, and Lucia—" anxiety grasped her heart as she considered the woman who'd raised her. "She's still there."

He looked at her, his gaze serious. "Trust me, Lucia knows exactly what she's up against, and how to fight them. She'll be all right."

"What exactly is she up against?" Emma pressed. "I have a right to know." She looked over her shoulder into the back seat at her father.

"They won't bother her," he hesitated, then said, "It was you they were after."

The low timbre of his voice, the deadly sincerity of his tone, caught the breath in her throat. Cold fear flushed through her system, dampening her palms and the nape of her neck. "Why?" she choked, the word little more than a whisper.

"Because of your blood."

"My blood?" She stared at him, not sure she heard him right, but even as she tried to sort it out, to comprehend the meaning behind his words, pain twisted inside her. "You mean because of my family? Because I'm a McGovern?" Her stomach soured. What did her family lineage have to do with anything? "Tell me, please," she demanded, looking at him through the veil of her hair.

"No. Because of your *blood*." He grabbed her arm

where the vampire had scratched her with his long nails. "They're vampires. They want your blood."

"Vampires," she said, and something hysterical bubbled inside her. "All my life I've been warned by Lucia not to fall in love, that some demented gypsy witch had cursed my family. And every year, I've had to live in fear that the devil's wolves would come back just for me. And now you're telling me vampires are after me, too? What is this, some kind of freaking nightmare?"

"I'm sorry. But yes, your blood is different. What happened when you were a child, with the wolves, it changed you. It's made you…different."

"You mean when the wolves bit me?"

"Yes. We need to know why they bit you. What happened that night?"

She looked at him, at the eeriness in the dashboard lights playing across his face, and the haunting depths of his tone. *What happened that night?* She remembered her mother's tight grasp on her arm as she pulled her toward her, toward the wolves.

Bile rose in the back of her throat as memories bombarded her. Blood. Death. And the evil glow of red in her eyes. "Please, stop the car," she insisted, and clutched the door handle as the car slowed. She remembered Mr. Lausen's blood, dripping from his clutched fingers and running across the floor, racing toward her.

And something else. Some kind of darkness in her mother's widened eyes. She'd tried to get away, but the wolves—one of them knocked her down. It had stood over her and growled, baring its fangs.

Her stomach heaved. She covered her mouth as Damien veered the car to the side of the road, and skidded to a top. She practically fell out the door. As she vomited along the side of the road, she knew, without a doubt, that her nightmares weren't over, they were only just beginning.

The wolves had scarred her, they'd changed her, and now she was different. Yes, she knew that. She'd always known that. Tears spilled down her cheeks. The wolves had changed everything.

Five minutes later, after sitting in the grass on the side of the road trying to reach a state of calm, her stomach had settled enough for her to get back on the road.

"Will you be all right?" Damien asked.

She looked up at him and nodded, then tried to stand, but she couldn't seem to control the shaking in her legs.

Damien placed a steadying arm around her waist and helped her back to the car. "We won't let it happen, I promise," Damien said, and eased her into the seat— gently, as if she were a child, as if she were precious. He reached out and ran a finger along the scars on her cheek. "The Cadre will protect you."

She looked up into his eyes, so sincere, so full of caring and a dam inside her burst and her tears spilled over, washing down her face. "I wish I could believe you."

He gave her a solemn nod. "You will." Then he gently shut the door. He walked around to the driver's side, silently got in and pulled back out onto the road. "What's more, we'll teach you how to protect yourself. The Equinox is only two days away, and with its arrival, all hell will break loose on Wolvesrain."

Emma's eyes opened as she felt the car slowing. She'd taken his advice and slept. She'd had to. She couldn't continue thinking about everything he'd said, and what it had all meant. The trees parted and suddenly a castle perched on a small hill came into view. Moonlight gleaming off a river that flowed through the dense trees cast a preternatural glow on the stone peaks and turrets of the building. "Is that it?"

Damien looked over at her. "That's it. How are you feeling?"

"As well as can be expected," she muttered, distracted by the rabbits, at least she thought they were rabbits, chasing one another across the large expanse of lawn before disappearing into a thick forest lit by a rainbow. She blinked and the rainbow was gone. She shook her head, sure she must be mistaken, then gasped. "Is that a...no, it couldn't be."

"There's a lot of old magic in this area," Damien said, the corners of his mouth twisting into a smirk. "And not all of it is harmless. It's important to stay within the grounds of the castle. Don't venture into the woods, no matter how enchanting the paths may look, no matter how strongly you feel the call to wander along the water's edge. Humans don't stand a chance in St. Yve Wood after dark."

"Humans? What do you mean? What will happen?"

"Evil," he muttered under his breath.

Emma swallowed.

"Mischief. Foul play. Whatever you want to call it. People don't always come back from St. Yve Wood."

"Great," she muttered, as they skirted a large pond, crossed a small stone bridge and followed a pebbled road up toward the castle on the hill. "As if vampires and demon wolves aren't enough, now I'm driving through haunted woods."

"Enchanted," he said softly.

"What?"

"Not haunted. More like enchanted."

"I see. Thanks for enlightening me." They turned a bend and stopped before a large iron gate behind which sat a small white cottage covered in thick vines of red roses.

Damien let out a soft curse, then blew the horn.

Emma leaned forward to get a closer look at the cottage's gingerbread trim through the dim coach lamps on either side of the door. "It's kind of cute," she said, not knowing what she expected.

No one answered the blare of their horn, and the gate before them stayed shut. Damien hit the horn again, and held it until finally the door opened. A sweet-looking elderly woman stepped out onto the porch. She held up her hand to shield her eyes from the glare of the headlights.

Damien didn't turn them off. Emma looked over at him, confused by the hard line of his jaw, and the animosity on his face. He was looking at the sweet old thing with pure hatred in his eyes.

"What's the matter?" she asked, and was almost afraid of his answer.

"Nothing," Damien muttered, then said something under his breath she didn't quite catch.

The woman approached the iron fence beside the cottage and reached high into a tangle of jasmine vines. A small gate opened. She walked through it and toward the car. Damien rolled down his window halfway. The woman stepped right up to the glass and peered inside. Her gaze took in each of them, passing over Damien, her father, before finally resting on Emma. "What is the purpose of your visit?" she asked, looking over the rims of her spectacles.

The poor thing was still in her nightgown and nightcap. "We're so sorry," Emma started.

"You know why we're here," Damien interrupted. "Nica told you we'd be coming. Now open the gate and let us in."

The woman's eyes narrowed, became dark slits in the folds of her face. "Watch your tongue, dark one." Her spectacled gaze held his for an uncomfortably long moment before she turned to Emma and smiled.

With her soft gray curls and deep crescent-moon dimples, she looked harmless. Almost. "What is your business at St. Yve?" she asked.

"My father needs medical attention," Emma said and gestured toward her father in the back seat. "The Cadre has offered to help."

"Yes, he certainly needs it. Has the mark of the devil, he does. In fact, you all do." She wrinkled her nose. "I can smell it on you."

Emma frowned. "Excuse me?"

"It's all right, Ophelia," a man's voice called from inside the cottage. He stepped out the door, hunched over a cane, and wobbled toward them. "Ms. Barrows just called and authorized their visit."

The older woman's eyes narrowed and, for a second, Emma could have sworn they flashed green. She shook her head. She must be more tired than she thought.

"They've made the appropriate accommodations," the man continued, his voice rasping and barely audible. He stopped as a violent tremble shook him from head to toe. Emma gasped, afraid he might fall, but then the tremors stopped, and he carried on his way again, heading for the small opening in the fence.

"Never tire of the games, eh, Ophelia?" Damien sneered. "You must get awfully bored. I know I am."

"How is that lady friend of yours, dark one? Still languishing away up there in the stone keep?" She leaned forward, a twinkle in her eye, her tone delightful. "Is your heart still attached to hers, growing weaker day by day, fading with each passing moon until it becomes nothing but a shadow of what-could-have-been?"

Damien didn't move. Not a muscle, not an eyelash, but his knuckles whitened as he grasped the steering wheel. Emma wondered what "lady friend" the woman was referring to.

The woman laughed and suddenly she didn't sound so old, nor did she look so frail. "Ah, maybe I'll start calling you 'regretful one.'"

"Are you going to let us through or keep wasting our time with useless chitchat?" Damien asked through gritted teeth.

"Come, Ophelia," the old man said, as he finally reached them. "Let them through. Their troubles have only just begun. Can't you smell it on them? Death and fear—" he made a breathy noise as he loudly inhaled the air. "Sickly sweet." He grinned, his skin stretching into something hideous over his large yellow teeth.

"And that one," he said, gesturing toward Emma with his trembling rheumatic fingers "She has the essence, flowing in her blood."

She started to shake at his words, a slow tremble that moved up her legs and encapsulated all of her.

"All the more reason to send her packing now," the woman said with a small rasp.

Emma stiffened, pushing herself back into her seat. Who were these people?

"That's enough," Damien barked. "Now, open the gate, or you'll both be feeling my essence."

The woman's paper-thin lips shut tight. "Don't threaten me, boy. I used to eat your kind for lunch. Bloody parasites. You serve no useful purpose in the world." She twisted her mouth into a smirk. "You're not even pretty to look at."

"Let's go, Ophelia." Her husband grabbed her by the arm and turned her back toward the cottage, took two steps then stopped as another bout of shaking took hold of him.

Emma let out a deep breath as Damien rolled up his window. "They are…horrible," she said, and tried to calm her fluttering nerves.

"They're the estate's threshold guardians," Damien explained. "It's their job to keep out *undesirables.*" The word caught on something in his throat.

"Undesirables? Then why were they so interested in us?" Emma asked, and noticed that the man's shaking suddenly stopped and he stood straighter, growing larger as they drove through the gate. He smiled widely and waved to her, the gesture nearly stopping her heart, as if he'd reached deep inside her chest and crushed it within his frozen bony grasp.

She patted her chest and took a deep breath, then turned to ask Damien to explain why they would be so undesirable, but stopped as they drove through the gates. Her breath caught in her throat and all words escaped her as she took in the magnificence of the estate.

Before them, the moon's reflection shimmered in a large oval pond surrounded by a lush emerald lawn. A lone swan drifted majestically across the water's rippled surface. Wonderment filled her as her gaze drank in the beauty. No detail was spared, down to the carvings in the intricate stonework of the castle walls, the peaked roof complete with iron adornments and ornate balustrades surrounding open-air balconies and square towers.

Never in her wild imaginings could she ever have

pictured any place more beautiful. "It's incredible," she muttered.

"We're approaching the entrance to the main part of the estate where the family of the Earl of St. Yve lives. The Cadre entrance and the hospital wing is housed around back," Damien said as they followed a cobblestone road up to the large castle.

They drove up to a porte cochere flanked by two large stone gargoyles whose ribbed wing tips expanded a good ten feet across the road, creating an almost menacing arch for them to pass under. Emma quickly rolled down her window, then stuck her head out and peered up at the gargoyle's wings as they passed beneath them.

She smiled in amazement at the fine details carved into stone—long veins and sharp bones jutting beneath sinewy muscles stretched taut. She looked up into the beast's eyes, and they blinked, their inky blackness focusing on her. Emma gasped, and dropped back into the car so fast, she hit her head on the roof.

"What is it?" Damien asked, a trace of a grin twisting his lips.

She glanced behind her, but saw only cold, hard eyes of stone. "Nothing. I'm sorry."

He looked at her, eyebrows cocked.

"This place is like something out of a Grimm Brothers fairy tale—fantasy with an underbelly of malice."

He nodded. "That's one way of putting it."

"Do you have another?"

"Not one I'd mention in front of a lady."

She saw amusement twinkling in the corners of his eyes, and wondered if this was all just a dream, a twisted terrible dream.

"Don't worry, this night will end."

"And then where will I be tomorrow?"

"Ah, the portrait of tomorrow depends on choices we paint today."

She stared at him, her mouth twisting into a smirk. "Great, I've been rescued from vampires and demon wolves and delivered to an enchanted creepy castle by a very strange poet."

He took a deep breath, and parked the car. "All in a day's work. But don't worry, we won't let you get too comfortable, your time has only begun."

Her chest filled with dread. "I'm afraid to ask."

## Chapter 8

As they parked the car two footmen, waiting with a gurney for her father, rushed forward. Emma bit her lip and squeezed her dad's hand as they secured him onto the gurney. Without saying a word to her, they hurried him inside. Emma took a step to follow, but Damien stopped her with a gentle hand on her arm as a tall, exquisitely dressed woman approached.

"Hello, Damien," the woman said, and leaned in to air-kiss his cheek.

Emma felt him stiffen next to her. She didn't know what she'd expected on the drive to St. Yve, but it wasn't this woman with her silk pantsuit, perfectly coiffed hair and impeccable makeup in the middle of the night.

"Welcome to St. Yve," the woman said and held out a long, slender hand with polished red nails. "I'm Nica Barrows. Anything you need during your visit I'm here to help you with."

"Thank you," Emma said, shaking her hand. "But the only thing I need right now is to see to my father."

"Of course. That's perfectly understandable. Let's give the doctors a little time to finish their examination, then we'll see what we can do."

Emma stared at her for a moment, feeling slightly off-balanced and confused by her frosty demeanor. "But don't you need me to talk to the doctors, to give them my father's medical history? How can they possibly help him, or understand what happened without talking to me first?"

Ms. Barrows clasped her hands in front of her, and straightened her shoulders, making them even squarer than Emma thought possible. "No need," she said in her ultra-smooth tone. "We've already contacted Dr. Callahan and have all his paperwork on file. We've also spoken to Ms. Lucia and she filled us in on what happened at Wolvesrain."

Emma's heart squeezed painfully in her chest. "Lucia? You talked to Lucia?" Would Lucia talk to the Cadre? The very people she had spent years admonishing? Emma turned to Damien, the question clear on her face. He only shrugged, which didn't help any. So much for her grand poetic rescuer.

"Don't be alarmed," Nica said gently and offered a smile, but the smile didn't reach her eyes, and didn't offer Emma a smidgen of comfort. "I know it's hard to believe or even comprehend," she continued, "but we've been keeping extensive records on your family for years. We have everything we need to help you, to keep you and your father safe."

Emma stilled. She looked from Damien to the woman, then back to Damien again. But found no answers from him. What did she mean, they'd kept records for years? Had Emma made a mistake? Should she have turned her father over to the Cadre? Should she have even come to this…this place?

She thought of the spiky-haired man pulling her out of Damien's car, the snarl on his face, the monster sheen in his eyes. Damien had said he was a vampire. A vampire! And what about Ophelia and her whacked-out husband, or the gleam in the gargoyle's eyes, had she imagined everything? Had she finally lost her mind, or was her world really coming apart and she needed them to help her…to keep her safe?

Her vision darkened around the edges, and her stomach did the flip-flop dance, once more threatening to spill. Her knees buckled. Damien grabbed her around the waist, and easily lifted her into his arms. She leaned against his hard chest, hearing the soft thud of his heartbeat, smelling the richness of his scent, feeling the warmth of his skin. God, she hoped she was right, and she could trust him. She wanted so badly to, more than she'd wanted anything.

"We've had a rough night," Damien said, and stepped forward toward the castle. "Emma needs to rest. Can we do the interrogation in the morning?"

Emma brought her arm up and wrapped it around his neck. *Interrogation?* Was that what was happening here?

Ms. Barrow's eyes narrowed. "Please believe that we have your best interest at heart, Emma. We've been trying to break Camilla's curse and help your family for a long time."

Emma closed her eyes. Instead of helping, the woman's words sent a cold wave of anxiety washing through her. *Camilla's curse.* "I'm okay," she said to Damien. "You can put me down."

He did, and she reluctantly let go of him, then followed Ms. Barrows as she turned and walked toward the doorway they had taken her father through, the doorway that led into the bowels of the castle.

Damien pressed his hand to the small of Emma's back, the slight pressure urging her forward. Against the warning bells clanging in her mind, she allowed him to lead her inside the giant wooden doors and into Cadre headquarters at St. Yve.

The lobby of the castle was luxurious and lined with thick red carpet. The room was sparsely furnished in antique red velvet settees and chairs. Mahogany tables held Tiffany lamps that splashed a multitude of jeweled colors against the gray stone walls. Intricate tapestries were hung everywhere to warm the room, displaying scenes of enchanted forests and magical images of fairies and unicorns.

But Emma's eyes kept drifting back to the carpet and

the overwhelming color of red so deep it seemed to move, to ebb and flow, as if it were an organ, and she were standing in the beating heart of this castle.

She shook her head to try and dispel the image, but it stuck and with one leaden step after another, she followed Ms. Barrows up a wide staircase adorned with sharp pointed wrought-iron rails to the second floor and down another bloodred hallway.

Perhaps Damien was right. Perhaps she needed to rest. More likely she never should have come here in the first place, and she certainly should never have let her father out of her sight.

But before she could ask after him again, Ms. Barrows stopped before a door painted with an exquisite peacock, the delicate brush strokes detailing an array of gold, greens and blues. Breathtaking in its beauty, it would have been enchanting if it weren't for the bird's sharply pointed talons and hooked beak piercing a fat green worm.

"You both have been appointed guest suites," Ms. Barrows said. "Damien, yours is the dragon room, two doors down." Emma shuddered at the thought of what was painted on that door.

Ms. Barrows opened the door before them, displaying a lavish room unlike anything Emma had ever seen. She gestured them forward, and Emma stepped cautiously into the room, relieved that the dominant colors were blues and greens.

"Thank you, Nica," Damien was saying, but Emma ignored them as she collapsed into the nearest chair and closed her eyes. "Enchanted," she whispered. This whole place was an enchanted nightmare.

"We have a long day and a lot of work ahead of us if we're going to have any chance of beating this thing," Ms. Barrows was saying. "Try and get some rest."

Emma opened her eyes, and looked at her through fuzzy bleariness. "I'm sorry? What do you mean?"

"I know you don't know much about us and what we do, but we didn't just bring you here to save you from the wolves, or to hide you from the curse. We want to help you fight this evil, and we mean to succeed. To do that, we're going to need your help, and we're going to need you on top of your game, not dead on your feet."

Emma didn't care for her tone, nor the way the woman was looming over her.

"There's an old evil lurking at Wolvesrain," Ms. Barrows continued. "And we mean to capture it and keep it from ever coming back again."

"I'm glad to hear that," Emma responded, sitting up straighter and crossing her legs. "But I won't sleep and I won't help you until I know that my father's okay."

"And you will, tomorrow."

Emma's fists clenched at her sides. She narrowed her eyes and pinned the woman with a look she hoped would curl her toes. "No, I need to see my father, now. Then, and only then, will I help you." Emma's teeth hurt. She unclenched her jaw, but not for a second did she look away from Ms. Barrow's frozen gaze. She held it steady until at last the woman turned away.

"Very well, then. Follow me."

Surprised, Emma stood on wobbly legs. That went easier than she'd thought it would.

"Bravo," Damien whispered in her ear, his praise sending an unexpected flush of warmth to her heart. He patted her shoulder, then stepped forward. "Nica?"

The woman stopped and turned back to him, clearly annoyed.

"I won't be in need of the dragon room. If you'd call and give me access, I'll be collecting the demon-containment crystals and be on my way back to Wolvesrain."

"What?" Emma gasped, and grabbed his arm. "You're not staying?"

"You'll be fine," he said softly. "It's better that I go back alone. Nothing will happen to you here."

"Are you kidding? In this place?" She opened her arms wide, her shock raising the tempo of her voice to near shrillness.

He looked at her, the regret clear in his eyes, causing panic to swell in her chest.

"Please," she said. "This place is like something from a reaper's twisted dream. Don't leave me here alone."

He touched her chin, his thumb caressing her jaw. "I'm sorry. I must go. You will be okay here. I promise."

She jerked away from him as anger, hurt and betrayal melded and rose in her chest to choke her. He was leaving her in this nightmare alone.

"They will teach you everything you need to know. And I hope that if I do my job right you can go back home to Wolvesrain, and never have to worry about the wolves ever again."

"Or the vampires?"

He glanced at Nica, then turned back to her. "We can only hope."

She stared at him, then asked herself why she was so surprised. Why wouldn't he leave her? His job was to collect her and deliver her to the Cadre. He'd done just that, and anything she might have imagined was between them was just that—her imagination running overtime. Tears burned the back of her eyes. She was such an idiot.

How could she think they had something? That he cared about her? They'd only known each other for one night. One long, eventful night unlike any she'd ever had before. And if she were lucky, unlike any she'd ever have again.

"All right," Nica said to Damien. "But come with me while I take Emma to her father. Obviously there are some things we need to discuss before you go."

Damien searched her porcelain face, but couldn't discern anything from her expression. As usual. In order for her to display an emotion, she'd first have to be able to feel one. Something he'd never seen Nica do, unlike Emma whose every thought shimmered in her exquisite eyes.

Her misplaced trust and open vulnerability ate at him. He knew he could never offer her what she needed—someone to depend on, someone to be there for her. He'd been called a lot of things over the centuries, but a hero wasn't one of them.

He sighed. It was just as well Emma had become disillusioned with him now, because if she ever found out the truth about him, she'd run as far and as fast from him as she could. He followed Nica down one hallway after another, refusing to look at Emma again, to see the disappointment lingering in her eyes.

As they reached the hospital wing, he and Emma stood outside Mr. McGovern's door as Nica spoke in hushed tones to the nurse in charge. Emma fidgeted. He could feel her eyes on him, could sense the sadness emanating from her. She needed him to comfort her, to assure her that everything would be all right. And he wanted to give that to her, but didn't. He had to pull back. He only hoped, for her sake, that her father hadn't worsened, that the Cadre doctors had been able to determine what the wolves had done to him and how to help him.

Nica and the nurse gestured for them to enter, and they walked into Mr. McGovern's room. He was lying on the bed, an IV drip in his arm, an oxygen mask over his face. He looked small and vulnerable, a broken man. Emma let out a soft cry and ran toward him. Damien's legs twitched, but he held back. His first instinct was to move forward and help her, to offer her comfort, but he stopped himself.

He couldn't be there for her. Depending on him would not help her.

"I've called the doctor," the nurse informed them. "He'll be back in a moment."

Emma sat by the bed, her eyes large and wet. She took her father's hand in hers and squeezed it. It was a simple gesture, and yet it moved Damien. It had been so long since he'd cared for someone that much, and since someone had cared for him.

"Excuse us, Emma?" Nica said. "Will you be all right waiting for the doctor alone?"

Emma nodded and, for a second, her gaze caught his. She wanted him to stay with her. Her longing reached inside him and touched something he'd thought was dead. And as it jerked to life, he realized he wanted to stay with her, to be there for her. But he couldn't be. He had a job to do, and he would finish it. He wouldn't stick around and grow close to her only to see the horror in her eyes when she discovered he wasn't human.

He turned away from her and walked out the door. He and Nica walked down the hall in silence, each lost in their own thoughts. Damien knew she wanted to talk about the vampires. He wondered if the Cadre knew it was Nicholai out there, and if they had any idea how powerful he'd become.

Probably not. If they had, they would have gone after him. They'd hunt him down and confine him in their dungeons. While demons could be contained in crystals, or sent back to the dark realm, vampires couldn't. They had to be placed in stasis, and stored in chambers in the walls and floors.

He'd prefer death any day.

He sighed. One more thing he and the Cadre disagreed about. One more reason he had to leave here as soon as possible. He would go back and deal with Nicholai and Asmos, and he'd do it alone.

Nica turned, and he followed her down another hallway. "This will only take a moment," she said, and stopped abruptly, opening a door in front of her.

"What is this—?" Damien stopped in midsentence as surprise sucker-punched him.

*Cara.*

# Chapter 9

Pain, razor-sharp, sliced through him. She didn't look as he remembered. The image he carried of her in his mind was the way she'd looked the last time he'd seen her. She'd been beautiful, her cheeks full and rosy, her hair long and shining as it rested on her shoulders.

Now, she was pale and emaciated, a broken shell after her internal battle with the demon who had possessed her, and the exorcism that had left her mind shattered.

"Why did you bring me here?" he asked, his voice barely audible over the lump in his throat.

"We need to discuss her," Nica said matter-of-factly. As if Cara wasn't a person at all, but a business transaction.

"Why? Has something changed? Other than—" he gestured toward her "—the obvious?" Anger formed a tight ball in his chest.

"I know this is hard for you—"

"Hard for me? You don't know the half of it." He turned away from Cara, stepping close to Nica, towering over her. "I told you the demon was too strong, that we wouldn't be able to contain it, to capture it in the crystal. I told you we had to kill it. But the Cadre fought me every step of the way. And she paid the price."

Nica didn't flinch. She waited half a beat, then asked, "Was that demon stronger than Asmos?"

Damien hesitated. He wasn't so sure.

"Asmos and the demon who did this to Cara are both from the seventh realm, an elusive dimension we're just now learning about. They're both ancient demons. Very powerful, very strong. Too strong for you to battle on your own. We've learned that from what happened to Cara."

He turned back to his partner, knowing she'd never open her eyes and look at him again. He sighed. "What do you suggest?"

"You have to wait until Emma's ready, then take her back with you to fight Asmos."

He spun back around. "Are you insane? That wisp of a girl wouldn't stand a chance against Asmos. Hell, we barely made it out of there alive tonight as it is."

"We have to work together, Damien," Nica said, her voice unwavering. "The lone gunman routine isn't going to work this time. Not with Asmos."

His fingertips hovered over Cara's hair. The blunt edge of regret beat at him. "And you want me to bring an innocent girl into this fight?"

"She is the last in the McGovern line. She has to be there to draw Asmos out of the wolves, it is the only way you'll be able to capture him, in that split second between vessels."

"You know the odds of achieving that are next to impossible."

"For most demon hunters, but not for you, Damien."

"And if I mess up? If something goes wrong? He will possess her. If my timing is off, even by a second, her mind will be shattered by the hate, by Asmos's evil essence. It's not right to risk it, to risk her. Let me go it alone. I have nothing to lose."

"Damien, if you try to capture Asmos alone, you will die. And chances are that eventually he will possess her, anyway. This is the only chance you and Emma have. If you want to save her, save yourself, you will not fail." She turned and left the room, leaving him alone with proof that, in this game, things do go terribly, horribly wrong.

He pulled up a chair next to the bed and sat in it, staring at Cara for a long time. Watching the steady rise and fall of her chest. She'd been so lovely, so full of everything life had to offer. Now she was an empty shell, and it had been his fault. He'd been too late, his timing off. Now, they wanted him to do it again.

*If you want to save Emma, save yourself, you will not fail.* Her words mocked him.

Leaning forward, he took Cara's hand in his. Her skin was cool, her touch soft. He almost expected her to turn toward him, to open those beautiful brown eyes and smile. But she didn't.

Damien dropped his forehead to Cara's hand. He closed his eyes, as guilt and anguish washed over him. He thought of Emma, targeted by the demon of wrath to be his next vessel. Why? Because she was unlucky enough to be born a McGovern. If he failed again, what would happen to her soul? Would it be cast out, sent to some demon realm leaving her body half-dead yet still alive? Or would it be trapped within her, stuck while some monster used her body for his evil purposes?

His hands fisted as fury fueled him. He wouldn't let that happen. Not again. There might not be anything he could do to help Cara, but he wasn't about to stand by and let an innocent woman who hadn't chosen this fight play victim to Asmos any longer.

He grabbed Cara's hand again and squeezed it, then leaned close to her ear. "I'm sorry, Cara." He forced back the emotion stinging his eyes, then turned and, without looking back, walked out the door.

*Blood surged like a river, shimmering in the moon's light as it filled the crevices between the stones, flowing across the stone verandas, seeping down the castle walls, running in rivulets across the stone gargoyles to spew out of their jagged-toothed, snarling mouths.*

Emma sat straight up in her bed. Her breath, caught in her throat, choked her. The moonlight, streaming through the window, bathed her in its otherworldly glow. In the distance, she could swear she heard wolves howling, calling to her, beckoning her home.

The scars on her cheek burned.

She rubbed her arms, though there was no chill in the room. She stepped out of the bed, her feet sinking into thick gold carpet as she walked toward the window. She stared into the night, searching for the stealthy movement of the wolves, but saw no sign of them. She'd been dreaming again.

Somehow she'd thought that within the walls of St. Yve Manor she'd be safe, that she'd be free of the Curse, of the dreams. But they were still there, lurking in the deep recesses of her mind.

There was a soft knock at the door. Surprised, she switched on the light, and, pulling on a thick blue terry robe that hung in the closet, walked into the main room toward the door. "Who is it?" she asked softly.

"Damien."

His voice, soft and velvety, caressed her through the door. Her heart skipped a beat of anticipation as she finger-combed her hair and opened the door.

He stood leaning against the doorjamb, looking a bit worn and frayed around the edges.

"You're still here," she said, trying to keep the pleasure from seeping into her voice.

"Did I wake you?"

She gave him a wry grin. "No. Even here the dreams come."

"That bad, huh?"

She nodded.

"I wanted to let you know that I'll be staying a little longer. You seemed…upset earlier." He looked tired, defeated, his eyes not quite reaching hers.

"Is everything all right?" she asked.

"No," he admitted, surprising her with his honesty.

She stepped back, inviting him in. "What is it? Your lady friend?" she asked, thinking back to what Ophelia had said.

"No. Yes. I mean. Something's happened to her. She's in a coma, of sorts."

"I'm sorry."

He reached out and touched her hair, pulling it through his fingers as he stepped closer. She didn't move, though she longed to pull him into her arms and hold him. Not just for her, to feel the warmth of his arms around her, but for him. He seemed as though he needed it, as though he needed her.

Instead, she took a deep breath, inhaling the smell of him, pulling it deep inside her and locking it away. This way, after he was gone, she could think of him, she could remember the way he smelled, and the way he smiled when he looked at her.

But he wasn't smiling now.

"She was a demon hunter," he said, interrupting her thoughts. "Her last hunt didn't go all that well."

"Demon hunter." The words caught and tripped across her tongue. "Are there that many out there? Demons, I mean?" Somehow she didn't like to think about that.

"More than you could imagine."

"Oh." Her stomach twisted.

"Not all are evil, some are just plain bothersome. Some take enjoyment from our misery, some feed off our emotions and come when beckoned. Some, though rare, want what we have, a corporeal form, to be able to love, laugh and feel the sun on their face."

Emma stared at him, not knowing what to think. "And she hunted them? Demons?"

"Yes. Like me. We hunted them together. We were a team, but now...I work alone." He gestured her toward the sofa. "How much do you know about this place? About what the Cadre does here?"

She sat close and turned toward him. "Not much. They seem to want to help me. Though Lucia always blamed them for my mother's death, she never really said why."

"How much do you remember about what happened to your mother?"

Images flashed through Emma's mind—her mother smiling, grabbing her arm, pulling. Emma's stomach tightened. She closed her eyes and took a deep breath. "Not much."

He took her hand in his. She looked up at him, into his startlingly blue eyes.

"When we arrived at the gate tonight. The old couple—"

She shivered. "They were horrible."

"As I said before, they are threshold guardians. Their job is to make sure uninvited demons don't enter the estate."

"Uninvited." The word stuck on Emma's tongue, and soured.

"The man said I had the 'essence' flowing in my blood. What was he talking about?"

He took her hands in his, softly caressing them as his gaze locked on hers. His touch danced across her skin, warming her, making her breath quicken. She leaned deeper into the sofa, feeling slightly lightheaded. He scooted closer. She reached out her hand and placed it on his chest, not only to feel his warmth through the thick cable-knit sweater, but to steady herself.

"You can trust me," he whispered. "I won't let anything happen to you." He touched her neck, the softness of his fingertips raising tingles along her skin and to spread throughout her body, bringing a spike of pleasure to her center.

"What kind of spell have you cast on me?" she asked, her voice barely above a whisper.

"The same kind you've cast on me." His fingers moved up to her cheek, softly caressing the hardened scars left by the wolves' vicious bites.

She wanted to pull away, but couldn't seem to find the strength. More than anything, she wanted to lean into him, to press her lips against his.

"When the wolves bit you, they left something behind." The rich, warm timbre of his voice penetrated her mind, filling her with a soothing calmness that weakened her limbs.

"An essence," he continued. "It's how they always know where you are. It's how they'll find you when it's time."

What did he mean, an essence? Why did she keep hearing that word?

"The demon of wrath—Asmos. He lives in the wolves. He waits for the night of the Equinox, waiting for you to fulfill the curse and fall in love, to make love. Waiting for you to become his next vessel."

Her eyes widened as his words penetrated the fog in her mind. "Me? But why?" she whispered.

"It is the curse. You are the last in your family line. You are his only hope to stay in the mortal realm for good."

She pulled away and stood.

Standing behind her, he placed his hands on her shoulders, and leaned in close to whisper in her ear. "I won't let him have you. When the time comes, it's important that you remember to focus on me. On my voice. On my touch. I will save you. I will save us both."

She spun around. "But how? How can you stop him? How can any man stop a demon?" She wanted to laugh at the ridiculousness of it all, but couldn't.

"We will stop him together. You have his essence within you. I will teach you how to use it, how to make it your own."

"I am not a demon. I am not evil," Emma insisted.

"You're not evil because you choose not to be.

Humans aren't the only ones given that choice. We are all defined by our actions. That is what makes us who we are."

"Very well said, Damien," Nica said, walking through the door.

Emma turned, trying to hide her astonishment at the woman's arrival. "Doesn't anyone sleep around here?"

"I hope you don't mind, it was open," Nica said, and sat in the wing chair next to the couch.

"We do," Damien said, with a subtle harshness to his tone. "But don't let that stop you. So, did you hear every word, or just the ones that interested you?"

"Everything about the two of you interests me. And he's right, Emma, the choice is yours. You have the power within you to fight Asmos. Your destiny is in your hands alone. All we can do is help you."

"How?" Emma demanded. "I don't understand." Suddenly she was more certain than ever that she should never have come to this place.

"You need to tell us what happened to your mother. We need to know how the curse will be fulfilled, how the transformation will be completed."

Emma's stomach turned. "I was just a child. I don't remember."

"But you dream about it, no?"

Emma stared at her. "I won't go back there. I won't remember. I can't."

"You won't be alone. We'll be here to help and guide you."

"What difference does it make? It's in the past. My mother is dead."

"We need to know what happened to her before she died. We need to know the exact process. You need to remember, there can't be any surprises, nothing to trip you up, to distract you when you go after Asmos." Her voice was flat. No inflection, no emotion touched her face. "Try to remember what happened that night in the cellar. The night the wolves attacked you."

"No." Emma's voice was shrill, her hands clammy.

"Nica, that's enough," Damien interrupted. "We should leave. Let Emma get some rest." He placed an arm around Emma's waist, the gesture offering more comfort to her than she wanted to admit. She found herself fighting the urge to lean her head against his shoulder, to close her eyes and escape.

"You can't protect her from this, Damien. She needs to face the truth head-on. We can't help her if she continues to hide her head in the sand."

Wearily, he scraped his hands across his face. "I understand. It's just been a long day. For both of us."

Nica stood and took a step toward Emma. "I know this is a lot to take in so fast. But if you want to survive, you're going to have to tear down the walls you've hidden yourself behind. You're going to have to remember."

*No!* The protest rang through Emma's mind, and she squeezed her eyes shut, trying to block out Nica and the words she spoke, but she couldn't stop the memories as they rushed back. So much blood.

"You're going to have to face the truth. It won't be as hard as you think. The truth is right here." Nica touched Emma's chest, and as she did, something inside Emma broke.

## Chapter 10

The next day, Emma woke with a feeling of cautious expectation in her heart, and Damien's face in her thoughts. Her mind flitted over the way he had looked at her last night, the way he had touched her—caressing and gentle. And then she remembered the things he'd said, and an uneasy tremor moved through her. She turned and looked at the clock—2:12 p.m.

In no hurry to jump up and face what was left of the day, she looked around her at the large four-poster bed, the paintings lining one wall depicting little girls playing on a beach, the large plant in the corner, and the long silk icy-blue draperies shut tight across the windows. A beautiful room, in a beautiful castle, where darkness played in the corners.

For a minute, she wished she could close her eyes, and when she opened them again, she'd be back in her room at Wolvesrain, Lucia would be in the kitchen making breakfast, and she would never have heard anything about a curse or demons or vampires. Or Damien?

"Damien." She said his name out loud, rolling it around on her tongue, wondering what it would be like to be with him, to lie in his arms, to feel his kiss on her lips. He was the first man who'd ever looked at her with appreciation in his eyes. He didn't just see the scars on her face, he saw all of her, and whether or not he knew it, he made her feel beautiful.

Her stomach growled. She sighed and got out of bed, then shuffled into the luxurious bathroom. She stood in front of the mirror and looked closely at the three long gashes on her right cheek. Demon essence. She didn't feel it. Couldn't see it. And yet, it was there It made her different. And Damien thought she could use it to stop a demon.

"Wow, must be some stuff," she muttered aloud to her reflection. She turned and stared longingly at the large oval tub. Thirty minutes in that tub, and she'd feel like a new woman, but it was late, and she needed to check on her dad. With one last look at the gleaming porcelain, she stepped into the shower, quickly bathed and then dressed. Whatever was happening around them, her father's health was all that mattered to her right now. Damien or no Damien, if the Cadre couldn't help her dad, then she would pack him up and take him to see Dr. Callahan in London.

\* \* \*

Emma didn't know what she expected when she walked into her father's room, but seeing him sitting up in bed, a tray filled with his favorite foods on his lap in front of him, and a huge smile on his face, wasn't it.

A nurse, who'd been sitting by his bed, laughed at something he'd said, and stood as she walked in.

He saw Emma and waved her in. "Good afternoon, Emma."

"Hello, Dad," Emma said, feeling slightly confused. There was more color in his cheeks than she'd seen in a very long time. Whatever the Cadre was doing for him, it seemed to be working.

"Hello, Miss McGovern," the nurse said. "Your father is doing much better."

"I can see that."

"We'll have him back to his old self in no time." The nurse patted his leg and walked behind him to adjust his pillows.

Somehow Emma didn't think his heart could be magically healed after one day at St. Yve. "What do you mean, 'back to his old self in no time'?"

"I'm saying the doctor has ordered physical therapy. As soon as his muscles start working properly again, he should be able to get up and out of this bed and take me dancing."

"You'd better believe it," her father crooned.

The nurse smiled and pulled back his hospital gown to reveal a large bandage on his shoulder. Quickly and efficiently, she changed the dressing.

"What's that?" Emma asked, but as she looked at the suspiciously familiar marks, she already knew. Wolf bite.

"Some kind of scratch," the nurse said. "Don't worry, it's healing nicely."

"That doesn't look like a scratch." Emma walked around the bed to get a closer look.

Quickly, the nurse finished then covered it up, and pulled his dressing gown back into place. "Don't worry, Miss McGovern, we're taking excellent care of your dad." She smiled absently, then left the room.

"Hey, you chased her away," her dad complained.

Emma stared at him, feeling as though she'd just tripped and fallen down the proverbial well. "Well, I'm sorry, but I don't quite understand what's going on. That didn't look like a scratch to me. Why wouldn't she let me see it?"

"Who cares? I feel better than I have in years. Maybe just getting out from behind those dank old walls at Wolvesrain was all I needed. Now put a smile on that pretty face, and stop chasing off the nurses. I can't remember when I last had so much attention." He winked at her the way he used to when she was younger, and her heart softened.

She sat down in the chair next to him. Whatever the reason for his remarkable recovery, it was good to see him in such high spirits for a change. She leaned forward and spoke softly. "Want me to poke your toes with a needle? Give you a sudden pain, so you can call her back?"

"Ha! Very funny." He turned back to his food, separating the green peppers and onions from his potatoes. "How are you feeling?" he asked. "You look well. Not so mopey."

"Mopey? I'm not mopey." She shook her head and ignored his implication. "I slept well. I think." Truth was she didn't know how she felt or what to think. She picked up his orange juice and took a sip.

"Nightmares?"

"Not that I can remember. Though I'm sure that's about to change."

"Why?"

She sat quietly for a moment, not knowing where to start, not even sure what she wanted to say. "I'm sorry about what happened last night, Dad." She placed her hand on his arm. "I should have listened to you. I should have brought you here sooner." She gestured toward him. "Obviously, it was exactly what you needed."

But was it the Cadre that had helped him, or something else? She looked at the bandage on his shoulder. If one of the wolves had bitten him, would he now have "the essence," too? Would that account for his miraculous recovery?

She thought back on her own life. She'd never been sick. Not a cold, not a sniffle, not once. Lucia used to joke that it must have been because they were all so isolated out at Wolvesrain, but now Emma had to wonder.

Her dad picked up a piece of bacon and bit into it. "It's all right. The important thing is that we're here now. The Cadre can help us. They understand what we're dealing with. They've offered us a safe haven." He set down the bacon and looked directly into her eyes. "You'll be able to find peace here, Emma, if you let them help you."

The intensity of his gaze made her squirm, she stared down at her hands locked together in her lap. "I don't know, Dad. Something about all this doesn't feel right."

His mouth straightened into a thin line.

"They want me to remember what happened to Mum, to relive that night," she explained, expecting to see anger flaring in his eyes, but instead they filled with silent desperation.

"You need to cooperate with them. Give them whatever information they want."

Emma couldn't believe what she was hearing. "But you're the one who never wanted me to think about that night, let alone talk about it. Now you want me to open a vein and let it all spill out?" She rose out of her chair, pacing back and forth, as turmoil warred within her. She stopped, and grabbed the back of her chair to steady herself, took a deep breath, and said, "I don't understand."

"I'm sorry. I was wrong. I should have let them come all those years ago after your mother died. Especially after what happened to Mr. Lausen. If I had, maybe our lives would have been different."

"How can you say that? How can you think that after spending only one day in this place?"

"Because I know the truth now. It's all very clear to

me. You can never leave here, Emma. Do you understand? If you do, if you go back to Wolvesrain, *he* will
find you."

"He, who?" she demanded, her voice growing shrill.

"Sit down, Emma."

Reluctantly, she sat back in the chair, and wished
Lucia was here with her unwavering logic.

Her dad leaned forward and clutched her hand. She
flinched when he squeezed too tightly. "Promise me,"
he begged. "Promise me you will never leave. If you
do, if you go back, one way or another, the curse will
be fulfilled and you will die."

Stunned, Emma stared at him as she finally began to
understand. This was all about her. He was scared to
death for her. Why? What had changed? Gently, she
pulled on her hand, hoping he'd release her. "I can't
spend the rest of my life locked up in this mausoleum."

"Yes, you can," he insisted. "You can have a life here.
I can't lose you, too. Do you understand, Emma?"

His words, the dead certainty in his gaze scared her
more than anything she'd ever felt before. What did he
know?

"What is it really, Dad? What aren't you telling me?"

He looked down, his face grim, his mouth closed.

"I'm sorry, Dad. I won't promise I'll stay here. I'm
not going to live my life in hiding." She stood.

"Wait."

She took a deep breath, and steeled herself for what
was coming next.

"How much of that night do you remember?"

She looked at him, but refused to answer. She wouldn't go there, not with him, not with anyone.

"Emma, we need to know."

"Now it's *we?*"

"Don't argue semantics with me, and don't be stubborn to the point of stupidity."

"Fine. Not much, okay?"

"But you have your dreams."

She sighed. "All the time. So much, in fact, that I can't tell the difference anymore between what are memories and what I've dreamed. I can't tell Nica what happened, because I'm just not sure."

"Maybe we can remember together," he said, softly.

For the first time in a long time, she saw the pain in his eyes. And she had to wonder what he thought of what had happened, how much he had seen, how much he knew.

"I do remember Mum speaking to me. I'm not sure when, because I can only see her face, but I think it was right before she died. She told me never to fall in love. She told me to break the curse. She made me promise."

He nodded. "I remember."

"Were you there, because I really don't understand any of it? What does falling in love have to do with anything?"

He sighed and leaned back against the pillows. "Falling in love is the answer to everything. People live for love, they die for love. Love is what makes the world go round."

She thought of Damien, and immediately pushed him from her mind. What did she know of love? She'd spent her whole life at Wolvesrain and could count on two hands the number of people she knew. It was only natural that she would apply romantic feelings to the first man who had ever shown an interest in her life. Acting on those feelings, or even believing in those feelings, would be a huge mistake, and lead her to nothing but heartache.

"So many people live their lives in fear," he said. "They're afraid of love, of letting go and opening their hearts. They try so hard to rationalize and control their emotions that they never allow themselves to be truly happy. Your mother was one of those people. Don't live like that Emma, take a chance on love."

Emma's eyes widened. "But how—"

"Okay, Mr. McGovern," the nurse said walking back into the room. "It's time for your physical therapy."

"Are you going to be the one massaging my poor withered muscles?" he asked with a wicked smile.

She laughed and took the tray from his lap. "You are a devil." She pulled a wheelchair from the corner of the room and helped him out of bed and into the chair. Before wheeling him out of the room, the nurse turned to Emma. "The dining hall is down the corridor to the left, if you're hungry."

Emma nodded. "Thanks." Though she didn't think she could eat, she ventured down the corridor, looking for the dining hall just the same, thinking about Damien. She wasn't sure how she felt about him, but they did have a powerful connection. Perhaps she should take a chance, push it a little to see how far it went. One thing she knew for certain—she wasn't ready for him to walk away. That alone should tell her something.

"Oh, there you are," Nica said, rounding a corner and breaking into her thoughts. "I'm glad I found you. Are you ready for your first training session?"

Emma stared at her, her eyes wide. "Training session?"

Emma followed Nica into a grand room, which very well could have doubled for a chapel. The stained-glass windows inset into the walls on either side of the room depicted scenes of various religious beliefs throughout the centuries. In addition, several museum-quality tapestries lined the walls.

Breathless, Emma was particularly drawn to the intricate design and colors of the one titled *Wheel of Becoming*. She could have stood there for an hour gazing at the fine details and brilliant colors.

"Beautiful, isn't it?" Nica said. "The wheel is divided into six realms of existence—the worlds of the gods, demons, humans, animals, ghosts and hell."

"Fascinating," Emma murmured, thinking the gods looked more frightening than the demons. The thought chilled her as she moved on to the next tapestry, this one a large disc etched with abstract symbols and various animals.

"This one displays the ancient theme of universal concord uniting heaven and earth and was used a guide for human life," Nica explained. She moved forward and pointed to another. "The Chinese believe there are five elements—wood, fire, earth, metal and water. The wood kindles the fire as it's devoured, the fire creating ash and generating earth, the earth producing metal within its rocks, and the metal secreting or attracting dew, which in turn enters the plants to produce wood."

"I see." But Emma didn't see. What did all this have to do with her training?

"It is with these elements that you will learn to fight Asmos. With the earth and water, you will learn to sharpen your focus." She pulled a beautiful necklace from her pocket. At the end of a long gold chain hung an intricate Celtic amulet carved from wood and ingrained with silver.

Nica placed the necklace into Emma's hand. "You will use silver and ash wood to protect yourself, and you will use the minerals of the earth in the forms of the crystals. But most of all, you will use your desire to triumph over evil, your determination to succeed, to fight this demon."

Stunned, Emma stared at the necklace, holding the delicate charm in her palm, then looked up at Nica. "Then I'm a lost cause."

Nica placed a hand over hers. "No, yesterday you were a lost cause. Today we're going to teach you how to have a future." Nica continued her tour of the tapestries until they reached the far end of the room where she turned back and gestured widely. "Everything in this room carries deep historical significance. Our people have been collecting these items through the ages, keeping meticulous records of man's spiritual journey across the centuries and continents."

Emma looked up at the soaring ceiling where arched crossbeams, stained dark walnut, crisscrossed the room, but couldn't find anything to say, other than to ask the question that had been plaguing her since this whole nightmare began. "Why?"

"So we can better understand demons and the role they play in the human realm," Nica said.

Emma nodded, but the answer didn't make her feel any better. Why were there demons here in the first place? Where did they come from? What did they want? As she pondered the questions, she realized these must have been the same questions the Cadre asked themselves when they'd started their foundation. The real question, then, the one that really mattered, was why her?

"But how is any of this going to help me fight the demon at Wolvesrain?"

"Everything we have learned since Camilla first summoned Asmos and cursed your family has convinced us that there is a way to fight him. It's all a matter of timing."

"But what about the vampires? How can we fight them, too?"

Nica stiffened and paused a second before she said, "Very carefully."

Emma wanted to say something but had to swallow over the large lump in her throat. "I'm still not quite sure I want to believe there are such things."

"Don't be surprised. Vampires are closer than you think," Damien said, as he walked through the door.

He was smiling at her. Not a big, wide knock-you-off-your-feet smile, but a small, intimate smile that made her feel it was meant only for her.

"What you need to know is how to neutralize one," Nica said, cocking one perfectly arched brow at Damien.

"Which wouldn't be nearly as easy as dusting one," Damien responded, dryly.

"Which would go against the Cadre's beliefs," Nica reminded.

"Yes, 'Do no harm.' I know. How can I ever forget?" he asked with a vicious undertone of sarcasm.

Emma stared at the two of them, and took a step back. The undercurrent of hostility in the room was making her more than a touch uneasy. If they couldn't agree on how to handle the vampires, then where did that leave her?

"Damien, perhaps you shouldn't be here," Nica said with a touch of a warning in her voice.

"I'll play by the rules. Promise," he said with a wink, then turned to Emma.

Drawn to the deep blue of his eyes, Emma felt momentarily mesmerized. She was entranced with the huskiness of his voice, the strength with which he carried himself, his utter confidence that he was right. As she stared at him, the walls around her fell away, and all she could focus on was him.

"Uh-huh." Nica cleared her throat.

Reluctantly Emma turned her attention back to the woman. She stared at her for a minute, before she realized Nica's silence was meant for her. "Okay. I get it. Focus."

Nica rewarded her with a smile, and Emma realized that was the first time she'd ever seen the woman smile.

"Okay, Paul here is going to start by showing you a few basic martial arts self-defense moves," Nica said. "You don't have a lot of time, so we're going to give you the condensed version."

Emma turned, slightly surprised to see a dark-haired Asian man in loose black clothing standing behind her. Not only had she not heard him approach, she hadn't even felt his presence.

"Paul," Damien said, nodding a greeting.

Paul nodded stiffly, then turned back to Emma.

"After that, he will demonstrate how to use the different types of elements shown around the room." Nica walked over to a display cabinet in the corner filled with various rocks and crystals.

"We've found that certain rocks have special abilities. Heliodor, for instance, helps enhance one's intuition. This one is hematite." She held up a large black crystal and handed it to Emma. "Ancient superstition says that large deposits of hematite were formed by spilled blood from battles that seeped into the earth. That's why when hematite is ground into powder, it takes on the color of blood."

"Lovely," Emma said, and handed her back the stone.

"We've found the best way to stop a spiritual being is with a natural element." Nica pointed to an odd-looking wand with a triangular bladed quartz for a tip. "That is a P'ur-pa. An ancient 'magic' deified dagger used for stabbing demons and exorcising evil."

"A demon dagger?" Emma asked in amazement.

"Yes. Unfortunately, most possessed humans did not survive the procedure."

"I can see why."

Next Nica took a milky-white pyramid-shaped quartz out of the cabinet and held it out to her. "Today, we use a different method."

Emma took the stone in her hand and stared at it, waiting for something to happen. Nothing did.

"It's a casting stone. Usually one has to be born with some sort of magic ability to be able to use and control the stones. You will be able to because of the demon essence coursing through your blood. We will show you how to harness that energy, how to make it your own."

"I still haven't gotten used to the fact that I have this...*essence.*"

"It's a part of you. Don't turn away from it. Embrace its power. Make it your own."

Emma nodded, though she really didn't understand what power she had. She certainly didn't feel powerful.

"How much do you know about magic?" Paul asked, stepping forward.

"It's all right, Paul," Damien said, before Emma could answer. He looked very casual leaning against the wall

Cynthia Cooke 159

with one foot kicked over the other, and yet something about his posture, about the way he stroked his jaw deliberately with two long fingers, revealed he was anything but casual. "I will train her."

Nica looked doubtful. "I don't think so."

"I taught Paul everything he knows. He is still only an apprentice. I am a master."

*Master at what?* Emma thought, but didn't ask.

Nica's gaze narrowed. "Were," she countered.

"Am."

"I won't risk Emma's life," Nica countered.

"That's good to hear," Emma added.

"I'm the best you have," Damien argued. "You know that. What's more, Paul knows it, too."

They turned to Paul and, reluctantly, he nodded.

"Very well then," Nica agreed. "As long as you abide by the Cadre's rules."

His mouth twisted into a smirk.

"And you're cognizant of the effect you and Emma seem to be having on one another."

Emma's breath caught and her cheeks burned. Were her feelings for Damien that obvious? She didn't even know the man, and yet, she couldn't seem to take her eyes off him.

"'Tis only the curse," Damien argued, which brought a slight frown to Emma's face.

"Is it?" Nica challenged, her chin lifting. "Not inside the castle walls it isn't. It's the two of you, and it will be magnified a hundredfold once you get back to Wolvesrain."

*You can never leave here, Emma. Do you under-stand? If you do, if you go back to Wolvesrain, he will find you. And you will die.* Her father's words rushed through her mind, and twisted her insides.

"Don't worry, Nica," Damien assured her. "We'll be able to fight it."

But even as he said it, Emma knew it wasn't true. He wouldn't be able to fight the attraction they had for one another any more than she could. There was something powerful drawing them toward one another. Even here within the walls of St. Yve where they were supposed to be safe, she could feel it pulling at her, pushing her toward him.

"What makes you so sure?" Nica asked, as doubt crinkled her forehead.

"Because I, more than anyone else, understand the consequences of this curse. The consequences of love."

# Chapter 11

"When are you going to tell Emma you're a vampire?" Nica asked Damien as they stood against the far wall of the room, watching Emma practice her blocks and kicks.

"Wasn't planning to," Damien responded. Though perhaps he should. That would definitely kill the attraction they had growing between them. She would look at him as if he was a monster, and she'd be right. He *was* a monster, made to feed off human blood. He had to fight the beast within him every day. And he was growing weary.

"Do you think that's a good idea?" Nica asked with one perfect eyebrow arched as her cold gaze drilled him. "I can see it causing nothing but problems for you."

He pierced her with a penetrating gaze. "Since when does it matter to the Cadre what I think?"

"It does matter, it always has."

Damien closed his eyes as frustration surged through him.

In an uncustomary gesture, Nica touched his arm. "You have been a part of the Cadre for more than two hundred years, Damien. We understand you're upset about what happened with Cara, and you have every right to be. We know how much she meant to you, and how much you meant to her. But do you really think she would want you to live like this, in complete isolation? We are your family. We only want what's best for you."

Her words surprised him, but even more surprising was the emotion behind them. It was so unlike her, and yet, he could hear the sincerity in her tone, feel it in her heart. He gave her a weak smile. "I appreciate that, Nica."

"I—we appreciate your help with this matter. More than I think you realize."

He nodded and, for once, was at a complete loss for words.

"I'm afraid if you don't tell Emma about yourself, and something goes wrong…" She looked down, then back up into his eyes. "We can't afford any surprises. The last thing Emma needs is to come face to face with your fangs in the heat of the battle. I don't think she could handle it."

He knew she was right. Emma would freeze up, at best. But in this instance, he wasn't so sure honesty was the best policy. "So you're agreeing there's going to be a battle. As in a war, a fight, heads are literally going to roll? That's a big step for the Cadre."

"We're not deluding ourselves about what you're going up against, and what you both have to lose."

"That's good." He thought of Charles Lausen, her father, and the way he had died. "You more than anyone else should be aware of that."

Her face fell, but only for a second. "I miss him. And yes, I want Asmos destroyed as much as you do. Make no mistake. It's just as hard for me as it is for you to trust that the council knows what they're doing. They've been at this for more than four hundred years. Sometimes we have to put our emotions aside and do what's best for the cause we work for."

Damien nodded, though he didn't wholeheartedly agree. He couldn't. He was the soldier in the field, he was the one fighting the battle. He and the other hunters put their lives on the line, so they could capture these paras and the Cadre could interrogate and study them. It wasn't the council who put their butts on the line, it was the hunters. And if a para had to die so a hunter could live, then so be it.

"Emma's beginning to remember what happen to her mother that night," he told her. "Soon the Cadre will have the answers they need."

"I hope so. It will eliminate some of the unknown factors and help you both prepare for what's coming."

He looked past her and watched Emma and knew Nica was right. As strongly as Emma was resisting remembering, they were in for a hell of a fight, and they couldn't go in blind.

"I'm sorry about Cara," Nica said. "There might be a slight chance…"

The old familiar pain twisted his chest. He turned back to her, refusing to let hope rise to the surface.

"Our interrogators have learned that Asmos is from the seventh realm, the same realm as the demon who possessed Cara. If you succeed in capturing him, our interrogators might be able to learn more about this dimension. They might be able to determine if there is any way to help Cara."

He quashed the fleeting spark of hope in his chest. "Ah, the proverbial carrot."

"The point is we just don't know enough about this realm to know for sure."

"And since we don't know for sure, it would be best if I follow the council's rules and not splatter Asmos into a million particles all over Wolvesrain's walls. Your interrogators could learn a lot from him, couldn't they?"

Her eyes narrowed. "Yes, they could. And it could also be true that I'm just trying to manipulate you. The question you have to ask yourself is, what do you believe in, Damien? Do you still believe in what the Cadre does? In our philosophy?"

"I believe in myself," he said, and turned back to Emma. "And in her. I'm not going to let her share

Cara's fate." He turned and caught Nica's gaze with his own. "No matter what it takes."

"I wish…" She didn't say any more, just shook her head and walked away.

He watched Emma move, and thought of what Nica had said. What if there was even the slightest chance she was right? That Cara could be saved? Emma caught his eye and smiled, and as she did, something moved within him, stealing his breath. She didn't deserve this. She shouldn't have to face what had happened to her mother and what was about to happen to her. She shouldn't be put at risk just so the Cadre could interrogate an elusive, powerful demon.

No matter what they could learn from him.

He walked toward Emma. "You look great."

"Thank you," she said, her smile broadening, reaching her eyes. His gaze zeroed in on the soft fullness of her lips, the small dimple in her cheek. More than anything, he wanted to pull her into his arms and crush his lips against hers. But that would be the worst thing he could do, for her, for himself. They both had to stay focused on the job at hand, and that was getting rid of Asmos. One way or another.

Then and only then could they explore whatever this was growing between them. He closed his eyes, knowing it was wishful thinking. As soon as she found out the truth about him, she'd turn and run. The temptation, the passion they felt toward each other would be gone. He should tell her. Now. Before things went even farther. But he couldn't bear to see the horror in her eyes.

* * *

Emma hit the ground hard, landing on her butt and skidding across the mat. "Ouch!"

"You lost your concentration," Damien said, his mouth twisting into a grin.

She glared as embarrassment flooded through her. "I can't do this," she grumbled, rubbing the sting out of her butt.

"Of course, you can."

"It's ridiculous. What do I know about martial arts?"

"Nothing. But by the end of today, you will be able to make a reasonable guess what I'm going to throw at you, and you will be able to block it."

"If you say so," she said doubtfully, then stood and faced him again.

He came at her. She stood in her stance, watched his eyes, watched the bunching of his muscles, his arms, his legs, where he positioned his weight, and this time she saw the kick coming, pivoted and blocked.

"Yes!" she whooped, smiling, then ended up on her butt again.

"Always expect more than one," he said and leaned over and offered an outstretched hand.

She took his hand and, as he helped her up, she turned in his arms, smiling, but the smile died on her lips as her eyes connected with his. He was so close his warmth seeped right through her clothing to tease her nerve endings. His raw power and male masculinity seduced her senses until her need for him to touch her, to kiss her was almost palpable.

And all she could think about.

He stepped back. "You're doing great, Emma."

Her eyes closed in silent mortification. "Am I?"

"Absolutely."

She took a deep breath to halt the flood of disappointment surging through her. Was she the only one feeling these emotions? They had a connection. He must feel it, too. "Listen, we've been at this more than three hours, I need a break," she said matter-of-factly.

He cocked an eyebrow.

"Don't look at me like that," she protested, and tried to keep the whine out of her voice. "I'm just not used to this much...training."

"Fine. We can spend some time focusing on techniques using meditation and the magical properties of crystals."

Emma groaned.

"Or we can start with spells, chants and rituals."

"I am not going to be able to do this, no matter how much training you give me. I won't be able to remember it all. I just can't."

He stepped closer to her, and her fool heart did a double beat. "Don't underestimate yourself," he said. "The first thing you need to learn is the power of positive thinking. You can do this. Now, I want to hear you say it."

"Oh, yeah, that will do wonders." She plopped back down on the mat.

"Say it."

She stared up at him, her mouth twisting into a

smirk. "Fine. I can do this. I can become the ultimate supreme demon fighter and clobber anything you throw at me."

He smiled. "That's better."

"I can feel it working already," she said dryly.

"We're going to have to do something about that sarcasm of yours."

"I like my sarcasm."

He sat cross-legged on the mat in front of her. "Emma, it's important that we trust each other. We're a team. We work together and, together, we can fight anything. You have to believe that, if we're going to make it through the Equinox."

She nodded, her brow furrowing. She needed to focus. She had to learn. He was right. What was important was their survival. She sat up straighter and wiped the silly pout off her face.

"We need to know exactly what's going to happen so we can plan our strategy."

"I'm not psychic."

"No. But you were there when it happened before."

She looked down. Not this again.

"Your father told us that he and Lucia heard you screaming. They went into the basement. Your mother was lying in your lap. She was dying. Do you remember that?"

She nodded, her face suddenly feeling as if it were drained of color.

"Emma, this is important. What happened to her?"

"I don't know," she whispered.

"Do you remember if she killed Mr. Lausen?"

She nodded. "I think she stabbed him. His blood, it went everywhere." She grimaced, remembering the image from her dream.

"She must have loved him, Emma, for the curse to have taken hold the way it did. She loved him and consummated that love. As she fulfilled the curse, enough of Asmos transferred into her so that she was compelled to kill him."

Emma shifted uncomfortably.

"Is that what you remember?"

Emma said, her voice cracking. "She grabbed my arm. I don't know what she wanted. She said I was the last one. She was pulling me toward the wolves."

He put his hand on hers. "It's okay. Go on."

"I don't remember anything after that, except before she died, she turned back into my mum again. She told me never to fall in love. To break the curse."

"Then however much of Asmos was in her, must have retreated back into the wolves. The first step was when she fulfilled the curse, falling for Mr. Lausen, then making love to him."

Revulsion filled Emma's face. "And if Asmos doesn't transfer? If I die before he can possess me?"

"Then it's over. You are the last. You are the one who has his essence."

"That's not quite true."

He looked at her, his eyes widening slightly.

"So does my father."

He took a deep breath. "I thought so. He healed too fast."

"We really don't know what's going to happen, do we?"

He shook his head. "No, we don't know what stopped Asmos twenty years ago. How your mother died. You were the only witness."

"I'm sorry. I can't remember."

"It's okay. The memories will come. In the meantime, we will have to proceed with what we know."

"Which is?"

"You already have the essence in you. On the night of the Equinox, we're going to try and draw him out of the wolves using the crystals."

The way he was looking at her, with desire alive in his eyes, warmed her, though she knew it shouldn't. She knew it should make her scared, should make her want to turn tail and run. But she couldn't help the joy surging within her. He felt the connection between them, too. It wasn't just her. He wanted her, too. "You think it will work?" she asked.

"I hope so. But we're both going to need to do it together. Two hands, two hearts, two minds—both focused on pulling him out of the wolves and into the stone. Do you think you can handle it?"

"I suppose. If I have to. After the last couple of days, I think I can handle anything. But tell me, why can't we train with real weapons? Wouldn't guns, knives and swords give us a better chance?"

"The Cadre believes in capturing paras. Studying

them, isolating them. Which is why I'm not teaching you how to protect yourself using weapons."

"But how can anyone think they can go against a demon without harming it?"

"Because we've been trained in other methods that have been proven more than effective. By using the demon-containment crystals we can capture a demon, then bring it back for the interrogators. They will conduct interviews and try to discover as much information about the demon as they can. Mischievous, trouble-making demons are debriefed, then deported back to the Dark Realm where they came from."

"And the others? The powerful evil types?"

"They're placed back in the crystals."

"Forever?"

He sighed. "Forever is a very long time."

"So, why do I get the impression that you don't agree with their choices?"

"I do and I don't. The problem is that the demons keep evolving and changing. And now it looks like there could be demons coming from a different demon realm, following different rules than the Cadre are used to. Up until recently, the Cadre's methods have always worked. We've been able to gather a lot of information, all to the benefit of mankind, information we wouldn't have if we had gone at this the way P-Cell does, blasting first, asking questions later."

"P-Cell?"

"They're known as death merchants. They're a secret paranormal task force division of the British Security

Service whose sole job is to hunt down evil demons and otherworld entities and eradicate them."

"Doesn't sound so bad."

"Yeah, except sometimes innocent people get caught in the crossfire. Not to mention that once a demon's dead, there's nothing useful that can be learned from it."

"But now things are different?"

He rubbed a hand across his face. "I've learned that there has to be a middle ground. Sometimes you have to bring out the heavy guns, or the price is too steep to pay."

The heaviness in his eyes concerned her. "Is this going to be one of those times?"

"It just might be."

"But if you go against the Cadre—"

"Then there will be no coming back."

She nodded, but couldn't help wondering what that would mean for her father. They'd made such progress with him. Could she chance them sending him away? Risk his recovery?

"Your forehead is creased with worry lines." He rubbed her skin with the pad of his thumb and smiled at her.

Her heart tripped, as she grasped for something to say.

"Let's practice our meditation," he suggested.

She nodded and he began to talk her through the relaxing ritual. Her mind focused on his voice, letting the rich timbre fill her until he was deep within her, and she was lost in his words.

"This is very important, Emma. When you feel you're coming apart, focus on my voice, on my touch.

That will be what pulls you off the edge. You need to trust me, totally and completely. No matter what."

"I do trust you," she insisted, but even as she spoke the words, a nagging doubt filled her mind, asking if perhaps her trust wasn't misplaced.

"You don't sound so certain," he said.

"I'm afraid."

"You should be."

The wall beyond it held the keys to her chains, hung side by side. To Wolfgang's surprise, you find yourself sitting on a floor that was sticky and dirty. A dusty, cobwebbed space.

"When you're ready," she said.

"I'm not."

"But how if I..."

*Chapter 12*

How could Emma tell him the truth? How could she explain that it wasn't her soul, or the demons, or even the vampires, as frightening as they were, that she was so afraid of—it was him. She was afraid that he'd already stolen her heart, and he was going to leave her, and take it with him.

She was afraid of going back to Wolvesrain, and living the way she had before. Alone, with nothing to look forward to, and no one to share her hopes and dreams with. To live like a ghost in a crumbling old castle.

"I'm not sure how you feel, exactly. I'm not sure what you want from me. Where you see this thing we have between us, going." There, she'd said it. She'd opened up, and told him her fears. And he did the worst thing he could do. He didn't say a word. Instead he got up and walked across the room. Disappointment filled her as she watched his retreat. Did he just not care?

He stopped in front of a cabinet and took out a large jagged stone filled with beautiful clusters of lavender and purple. She watched him with her heart lodged in her throat as he walked back and sat in front of her. He placed the crystal in her hand.

"This is called an amethyst. It will bring you inspiration and insight. Now look into the crystal, focus on the colors, on the movement within the stone."

She stared intently at the stone, trying to keep the tears at bay and concentrate as he asked, on the stone, on anything but the ache in her heart. But she couldn't.

"Trust me, Emma."

She looked at him, her eyes locking on his. "I want to."

"I don't want anything to happen to you. We have to concentrate on beating the demon. Then and only then, can we see about everything else. Okay?"

He was so practical, rational, logical. Male. She nodded. He was right. But even as she tried to do as he asked, tried to focus on the stone, she found her mind drifting. She closed her eyes slightly, peering at him from under her lashes, watching his every move, the rise and fall of his chest as he breathed, the slight tilt of his head as he concentrated on the amethyst.

She thought of the intensity of his gaze. The endless blue of his eyes that sent longing tripping down her spine.

Surely he could feel how much he moved her, and how much she wanted him to notice her, to think of her the same way she was thinking about him.

No, he was too busy focusing, or meditating, or whatever you called it. She wanted to know what it would feel like to be touched by him, to touch him. To be encircled in his arms and held close. How she wished she had the nerve to press her lips up against his, to—

"Emma?"

Caught. A guilty smile moved her lips.

"You okay? If you lose focus, you lose."

"I know," she whispered. There was nothing wrong with her focus, she thought, as she stared at his lips, his hands, the hard lines of muscles protruding from his sleeveless shirt. She just couldn't seem to focus on what he wanted her to focus on, on the crystal he was holding in his hands.

"Here," he said, and scooted behind her, nestling close to her back, too close. She could feel him all around her, his warmth, the hard lines of his chest. His scent drifted through her, teasing her.

He lifted the crystal in front of them. "Now take hold," he said softly into her ear, the rich tone of his voice reaching deep inside her to stoke fires already inflamed.

"Like this?" she whispered. She took a deep breath and held the crystal.

He cupped his hands under hers. "Now focus on the striations deep within the stone. Notice how they splinter, follow the shadows, then focus on the essence within you."

"Essence?" *Oh, God.* His breath, warm on her ear,

heated her skin and stole her breath. She couldn't move, couldn't concentrate on anything but his skin against hers.

"Picture it as a flower, a large white lotus sitting at the base of your spine. Now look into the crystal and picture the petals opening, one by one."

Her pulse thundered in her ears. She could barely hear him. Why couldn't she breathe? She let out a soft whimper, and turned slightly in his arms, her hooded gaze catching his. He stopped talking and stared at her, his eyes darkening with desire.

He did want her.

Her lips parted slightly, as she pulled in a shallow breath. He glanced down at them, then back up into her eyes.

She moved closer, her lips a breath from his. "Damien," she whispered.

And then his mouth was against hers. She wasn't sure how it happened, or who made the first move, but his kiss, his touch was everything she'd dreamed it would be and more. He moved slowly, tentatively pressing his mouth against hers. He tasted warm, his touch gentle. And then he pressed harder, and his hold on her body tightened, his lips moving over hers.

His tongue slipped into her, touching hers, moving back and forth, tasting her, sweeping inside her, as if he couldn't get enough. She let loose a soft moan, and swiveled so she could feel him closer against her, her arms wrapping around his neck, her fingers playing in his hair at the nape of his neck.

Warmth flooded through her, chasing a wave of euphoria. And after a moment she thought could never end, he pulled back and they stared into each other's eyes, neither of them saying a word.

"Well, there's a technique it appears she's mastered."

Emma stiffened as embarrassment washed through her. Damien pulled away and stood as a tall woman with long auburn hair and large green eyes stepped into the room.

"Lady Dawn," Damien said, nodding.

Emma didn't like the way she was looking down her nose at him, as if he disgusted her, and it was all she could manage to try and hide it.

"You must be Emma McGovern," the woman said, and held out a long, slender hand. "Dawn Maybanks. Nice to meet you."

"Oh," Emma said, standing.

"This is one of the Earl of St. Yve's twin daughters, and lady of the enchanted castle."

"You live here, then. In this place?" Emma asked, trying to keep the disbelief from her voice.

Dawn looked around her and smiled. "Yes, most of the time." She picked up the crystal off the mat. "Trying to teach her the arts?" she asked, casually. But Emma could see there was nothing casual about this feline.

"We're doing what we can," Damien answered.

"It took you years to be able to master the control of an adept. Why do you think she's any different?" Dawn said, gesturing toward Emma.

Emma stiffened and tried to stand taller.

"She has the essence," Damien said. "It's very strong."

"I'm sure it is, but not strong enough."

Damien sighed. "We're working on our positive thinking. You might give it a try."

Dawn looked surreptitiously around the room, then turned back to him and handed him a small bundle wrapped in an oilcloth.

Confusion lined Damien's face as he took the bundle from her. "What's this?"

"My father has issued orders for the vampire containment team to be deployed to Wolvesrain. You need to get there first and make sure there aren't any vampires left for the team to bring back here. Is that clear?"

Damien stared at her, his eyes hard. Then he opened the bundle. Emma inhaled sharply at the variety of weapons in his hand. Two wooden stakes, two silver daggers, and what looked like some kind of gun.

"A UV vamp blaster?" Damien asked. "The last time I saw one of these, it was aimed at me by some relentless P-Cell operative. How did the Cadre get hold of this?"

"It doesn't matter. I'm risking everything bringing these items to you. Now, do we have a deal?"

"I know you don't agree with your father's decision to entomb vampires beneath the castle, but this is a quite a bold step. The consequences if anyone finds out…" He shook his head.

Dawn smiled, but to Emma, the gesture appeared cold and calculating. *Don't trust her, Damien.*

"Don't worry about me, Damien. I know what I'm doing. In fact, you can think of it as a test if you want, of where your loyalties stand."

"What is that supposed to mean?" Damien asked, his face wary.

"Who are you loyal to, Damien? Cara? The Cadre? Perhaps from what I saw when I walked in, it's to this woman." Dawn gestured toward Emma. "Or is it your brother? Something for both of you to think about, eh?" She turned and breezed out of the room.

Emma stared wide-eyed at Damien. "Brother? What was she talking about?"

"I didn't think she knew. Didn't think any of them knew," Damien said under his breath as he picked up one of the ancient silver daggers.

"What does that mean?"

"It means there's more going on here than meets the eye."

"And?"

"And we'll have to be extra careful."

Anxiety twisted inside her. She stared down at the weapons, but somehow didn't feel better. "Wood and metal?" she asked, pointing toward the stakes and knives.

He sighed. "Yes, and a hell of a lot more useful on vampires than that trinket around your neck."

Damien felt the walls closing in around him as he dropped Emma's necklace, and watched as it nestled between her breasts. He knew this didn't bode well. Not for any of them, certainly not for Nicholai.

"What did Lady Dawn mean about not bringing any vampires back?" Emma asked.

"She doesn't like them."

"I gathered that. But really, Damien, who does?"

He looked down into her beautiful face, and knew he should tell her. Right then and there. She had a right to know who he was. What he was. The moment between them stretched, and though he knew he should, he didn't.

He liked the way she looked up to him. She saw parts of him no one else could, because all they saw were the fangs and the bloodlust and the constant reminders that he was just a ticking time bomb who might someday explode. And then he'd do what they'd all expect—he'd kill.

Instead, he held up the crystal in his hand. "We capture demons in containment crystals, then we house them in the dungeons below. By the thousands."

Emma gasped. "And vampires, too?"

"No. Vampires can't be pulled into the stones. The Cadre incapacitates them, then buries them in tombs in the walls and floor."

"Here? In this castle?" Emma's voice grew shrill, as she looked around her, and he couldn't help wincing at the horror on her face.

"Yes," he said, his voice soft.

Emma shuddered.

"I'm afraid that's how Lady Dawn feels, too."

"I can understand that. What I can't understand is why? Why keep them at all?"

"They use them as guinea pigs. Cadre scientists are constantly working, trying to find a cure to the vampire's bite." Damien swallowed his disgust, knowing that with one slip up, it could be him down there, entombed forever.

"Have they had any success?" Emma asked.

"No."

"So, I take it Lady Dawn doesn't agree with the process."

"No, but not for the same reasons I don't. She just wants them all dead."

"And you?"

"The Cadre policy of not harming is hypocritical. This place has become a para torture chamber."

Emma rubbed her arms, and looked around her, suddenly, looking very small and skittish. "Damien. I know I'm not done with my training, but I don't feel comfortable here. I didn't before, but now…now I feel like I'm ready to jump out of my skin. Do you mind? Can we go back to Wolvesrain?"

"It wouldn't be wise. Not now. Not yet."

"But—"

"Sit," he commanded, and sat back on the mat, then held out his hands to her. Reluctantly, she sat across from him and placed her hands in his. He closed his eyes, and walked her through the mediation process, talking her into a calm state, showing her how to control her emotions, her reactions. But he didn't do it for her, he did it for him.

He needed to block out her lovely face, the vulnerability swimming in her eyes, her need for him to be there for her. He knew enough about demon possession to understand that if Emma became a host for Asmos, her mind couldn't take the evil, the rage. Like Cara, she would be lost. And if she didn't learn everything he had to teach her, she wouldn't be able to withstand the seduction. The temptation of Asmos and the curse.

Hell, he wasn't even sure *he'd* be able to.

His most prudent course of action would be to take the weapons Dawn offered and go back on his own. The real questions was, why would Dawn go against the Cadre, against her father? Giving him weapons, giving him an order to kill vampires went against everything the Cadre believed in. Was she setting a trap? Trying to prove to them that he couldn't be trusted. That he was a born killer just as she'd always said?

He should leave the weapons there and walk out. But what of Emma? The two of them couldn't take on a vampire clan alone. Especially a clan that his brother was a part of. He could leave them to the containment team. The Cadre would love to study and dissect a vampire that fed off demon blood. As tempting as it was, he couldn't let that happen. He and his brother were fundamentally different on every level imaginable, but Nicholai was still his brother.

"Dammit," Damien swore under his breath. Emma's eyes popped open. He rose and turned away from her. Who was he kidding? He couldn't do this alone. Hell, he didn't even think he'd be able to pull this off if Cara were here. The thought of Cara, an empty shell lost to him forever, made his stomach clench.

"Damien?" Emma touched him lightly on the shoulder.

He turned around and stared at her. "You have to remember what happened to your mother," he said through gritted teeth. "We can't go back, we can't do this until we know what we're up against. We need to know what Asmos's weaknesses are." He grabbed her shoulders, wanting to shake some sense into her as her eyes grew large. "Tell me."

"I can't." She tried to pull away, which made him hold on tighter. "Stop!" She jerked free from his grasp.

He rubbed his hands across his face. "I'm sorry. I—"

She stepped close to him and wrapped her arms around his chest. "It's going to be okay," she whispered, surprising him.

He stilled for a moment, not used to the intimacy of the hug, the unsolicited affection, the friendship in her touch. "I hope so." He wrapped his arms around her and tightened the embrace.

"We have the weapons. We can manage," she said.

He stared once more at the weapons on the floor, certain that if he took them, he would prove to the Cadre what Dawn had always said about him. That he couldn't be trusted. That he might not be a killer yet, but it was just a matter of time. It was in his blood. It was who he was.

But if he didn't take them? And Nicholai and his clan attacked again? He knew enough about Nicholai to know he wouldn't stop 'til he got what he came for—Asmos's essence through Emma's blood.

He could get weapons anywhere, he even had a nice stash of his own, but for Nicholai he'd need something more, something stronger. He'd need P-Cell's vamp blaster.

"What about my dad?" Emma asked.

"He'll be fine here."

"Should I tell him we're going back?"

"If you come with me…" he couldn't say the words.

She nodded her understanding, and that kept him from having to say the truth, that there was a good chance she wouldn't survive the Equinox, and neither would he.

"He doesn't want me to leave St. Yve," she whispered.

"You don't have to. You can stay here. Spend the next year or two training, learning. Go back when you're ready. Asmos isn't going anywhere."

"And put my life on hold?"

He nodded, and swallowed the large lump in his throat.

"I feel like I've lived my whole life on hold. Waiting for something. Waiting for someone like you. I can't choose when or how I'm going to die, but I can choose whether or not to love." She looked up into his eyes.

He pulled away from her. This was a huge mistake. He couldn't let himself feel like this. Worse, he couldn't let her get attached to him. It would be cruel. To them both. "I'm not what you think I am. I can't be the one for you," he said, his voice breaking.

"But you already are," she insisted. "You feel what I feel. You understand me." She turned away. "You don't see a monster when you look at me."

Her words and the pain behind them twisted at something inside him. Gently, he touched her shoulder and turned her around to face him. "You aren't a monster. Nowhere near. You are beautiful."

She looked up at him with tears swimming in her eyes. "I've never felt like this before. Is it real? These feelings? Or is it the Curse?"

"I don't know," he said, and stepped back, trying to distance himself from the vulnerability and trust shimmering in her eyes. "It doesn't matter. Nothing matters right now, but capturing Asmos. Only then will we know what is real."

"Nothing?" she asked, her lower lip trembling.

He had to stop this, before it went any farther. He touched her cheek. "Falling in love with me is not something you want to do, not now, not ever. Unfortunately, I can't capture Asmos alone. And I can't stay here any longer. What we're going up against won't be easy, but if you choose to come back with me, then I'll meet you downstairs by the front door in twenty minutes." He turned and walked from the room.

## Chapter 13

The girl swallowed a giggle as she and the boy ran through the rain toward the barn. Her pulse pounded. Tonight they would sneak into Wolvesrain and take what they wanted. They'd heard the rumors in the village of the scarred girl who never left home, and the jewelry fit for a queen passed down generation after generation, sitting there gathering dust. Amy wanted some of those jewels. And John was the first boy she'd run across who was man enough to give her what she wanted.

John lit the lantern and put it on the floor. "Where'd this storm come from?" he asked, shaking his wet bangs out of his eyes.

"What's the matter, afraid to get a little wet?" she teased, and smiled at him as she rubbed her hands up under his shirt. She loved the adrenaline surge pumping through her veins. Loved the high she felt, knowing she was doing something just a tad wicked.

"I like it wet," he grinned, and took a handful of her breasts. She let him fondle her just long enough to keep his interest piqued and to keep him manageable.

"How much longer until we can sneak into the house?" she asked, tilting her head with a coquettish grin as she'd seen girls do in magazines.

He looked out the windows. "Let's wait a good half hour after the lights go out."

"That long?" She pouted. "What are we going to do until then?"

He smiled, and gave her ass a rough squeeze. "Take a guess, love."

She sighed and unbuttoned her pants. She was wet and impatient, and this old barn was rotted through and filled with spiderwebs. This jewelry had better be worth it, she thought and stepped out of her jeans.

Nicholai stood in the shadows of the barn and watched the show, feeling his cock stiffen as the boy smacked the girl's bare ass as she lay bent over a large hay bale.

"Oh, yes. Make me feel it," she squealed, squirming as her pale skin glowed pink with each slap.

Nicholai grinned as the boy hit her again, and dropped his pants to pool at his booted feet in the hay. She moaned with pleasure, and encouraged him as he roughly entered her, and pulled that glorious ass against him. John's thighs bulged, his buttocks squeezing, as he thrust his cock in and out of her, faster and faster.

The girl moaned, louder and louder. "Come on, baby. Right there." The boy smacked her again, and she screamed out loud.

Soundlessly, Nicholai moved toward the couple; they were making enough noise to mask any sound he might make. The grunting and groaning, mingled with the scent of their sex was definitely working on him. He wondered if they'd mind if he joined them? Not that he cared what they minded.

Nicholai smiled at the sound of the boy's hand connecting with soft, rounded flesh. He wondered if the girl would even notice if he took the boy's place and gave her the fucking she deserved. He stood behind them, watching the light from the small lamp gleaming on the boy's slick back, and unbuttoned his pants.

He stepped forward and cupped his hands on the boy's tight buttocks, and squeezed a handful. The boy froze, but before he could utter a word, Nicholai leaned forward and sank his teeth in the boy's neck, piercing his jugular and taking a long, sweet drink.

Nicholai reached out his hand and gave the girl's ass a randy slap, then bucked his hips forward, pushing the boy into her one last time, while he continued to drink deep.

"Don't stop now, you son of a bitch," the girl panted. "I'm so close."

When at last the boy was depleted, Nicholai pushed

him to the side, and shoved his hard cock deep inside the willing girl.

She groaned audibly.

He rubbed her sore ass and took his pleasure, easily lifting her up and driving deeper inside her. She screamed as the waves of pure bliss wracked her body, then she collapsed under him. It wasn't until he was done, and she was completely satiated in every way possible, that she noticed John's corpse on the ground behind her.

She turned and looked up at Nicholai, and then she screamed again.

It was very late when Damien and Emma finally arrived back at Wolvesrain. After saying goodbye to her father, Emma had cried softly, then had fallen asleep, leaving Damien to stew over what to do with her. He couldn't continue down this path. He had to get hold of his feelings for her, or they were both headed for a disastrous ride.

Her feelings for him were already too strong, sweeping him along in her current of need. It was powerful and addicting, but he couldn't be there for her. He wasn't the man she was dreaming of, that she believed him to be, no matter how much he wished he could be.

He parked the car before the darkened manor and turned off the ignition, then stepped out into the silent night. He stood there for a moment, reaching with his senses, searching for his brother, for the wolves. But felt nothing. All was quiet.

He walked around to the other side of the car and opened the door. He took a deep breath, stiffening his resolve, then picked Emma up, cradling her sleeping form in his arms, and carried her up to the house. Lucia, holding Angel in her arms, opened the door as he continued inside.

"How is she?" Lucia asked.

"She's fine. Just tired."

He could have set her down on the couch in the living room, could even have woken her to go up to bed on her own, and he knew he should have, even as he carried her up the stairs. But he liked the feel of her against him, her soft roundness, her delicate lavender scent. She needed him and, so help him, he needed her just as much.

How did that happen? How had she managed to get under his defenses? She saw the good in him, his strength, his humanity—the qualities no one else ever looked for. And he was too selfish to give it up, to tell her the truth and have that trusting look in her eyes fade into disgust.

He continued up the stairs to her room, knowing he had only a few precious minutes left with her before he had to go back into the forest and find his brother. He would attempt to make peace with Nicholai, to warn him the Cadre were on to him and would soon be there.

He carried no more illusions that he and Nicholai could reconnect, but ending up in one of the Cadre experiments would be a fate worse than death. He didn't want that to happen to his brother; no matter how many bad choices Nicholai had made over the years, he didn't deserve that.

He just hoped his brother would listen.

And quickly. Before the wolves returned. Before he had to wake Emma and start the ritual to try and draw Asmos into the crystals.

He laid Emma on her bed, and brushed her hair out of her face with a soft touch, then pulled the blanket up over her and tucked it under her chin. He stared at her for a moment, wishing he could lie down next to her, wishing things could be different. Instead, he turned to leave.

Her hand grasped his and drew him back to her. He turned to see her shining eyes opened and staring up at him. "Stay," she said, her eyes squinted with sleep.

"I can't," he whispered.

"Please. I don't want to sleep alone. I don't want the dreams to come back."

"But the dreams are good," he said. "They'll help you to remember. We need you to remember what happened to your mother."

"No. I don't want to remember," she said, her voice heavy with sleep as she pulled him down next to her.

"Emma, it could be the difference between whether we live or die."

Her face crumpled with pain. He sat on the bed. He'd stay just for a minute, he thought. What could happen in a minute? But as he sat there, smelling her delicate lavender scent, staring into her beautiful eyes, large and luminescent with the hint of the moon shining within their depths, he knew he didn't want the moment to end.

He saw himself within her. Like him, she carried so much pain and loneliness in her heart. She'd spent her life alone, longing for love. Hoping, but never believing it would come her way. But are these feelings they felt for one another real? Or was it the curse drawing them together.

She smiled up at him and, for a moment, he didn't care. He leaned down and brushed his lips against hers, liking the feel of their softness, their warmth as they opened beneath his. As his tongue touched hers, a spark of heat ignited in his chest. She tasted so sweet, like family, like home, like where he was supposed to be.

She let out a soft moan, the sound of it lighting the fires already stoked within him. His lips moved over hers. He closed his eyes and lost himself in the warmth, in the contentment he used to feel when he'd watch sunlight glint off a rushing stream, or ate strawberries while lying in the field of heather on a warm summer day.

What was it about her that she could rekindle all those feelings within him? She deepened the kiss, and he marveled in the gentle touch of her lips, the taste of her tongue, the quiet whimpering sounds rising from the back of her throat. And he knew he didn't want to be without her.

Not then, not ever.

Her palm pressed lightly against his chest as her fingers played with the buttons of his shirt. Her tentative touch lit the nerve endings along his skin, sending sparks rushing through him to chase away any lingering reservations. Gently, she scraped her nails across his chest, heating those sparks to a blaze of desire. He gasped, took her hand in his and gave it a gentle squeeze.

"Don't leave me, Damien," she whispered. No, he couldn't leave her. Couldn't imagine going back to the way it was before, when he was alone and life was so…empty. He had to take what she offered, he didn't have the willpower to turn away, to deny himself the one thing he's always wanted but has never been able to have.

Someone to love him.

He dropped his head to her neck, gently tasting her skin. He could hear her blood racing just below the surface. He ached to take just one sip, but knew it was something he would never do. Could never do. He'd never soil something so trusting, so vulnerable, so beautiful, with his monstrosity. Instead, he pulled her earlobe into his mouth and sucked gently.

She arched her back, and held him close, her fingers tangling in his hair. His desire ached. He had to stop this before it went any further and he lost all control. He sat up. So did she.

His eyes caught hers and he tried to form the words that would explain how he felt, and why they couldn't continue, but she smiled at him, her lips curving into a delicious half grin. Her eyes were heavy with desire and as her gaze caught his, she held it, held him, captive, then lifted her shirt up over her head.

He should go. Pull away and run. But he didn't as

she reached behind her and unclasped her bra. It fell away and he stared, mesmerized by her beauty, by the way the moon's glow played across her lush, perfect skin, by the enchanting gleam in her eye.

She took his hand in hers and brought it to her breast. He touched it gently, lifting its weight in his hand, caressing its softness. Heat rushed through his body, tightening his nerves. "I don't think—" his voice broke, rasping.

Before he could finish the thought, she leaned forward and kissed him, her mouth devouring his as their desire mounted. His thumb moved across her nipple, playing with the hard nub, so warm and pert beneath his touch.

He couldn't make love to her, he told himself. He wouldn't make love to her. But a part of him, hot and twitching, pushed relentlessly against his pants, aching to be free. And that part screamed louder than the rational thoughts trying to hold him back. That part of him wanted to feel her skin next to his, to feel her warmth. To bury himself deep inside her.

He pushed her back down on the bed, his body stretched out atop her, his erection nestling between the junction of her legs. He could feel all of her at once, and the sweet way she cleaved beneath his weight. And he had to have her.

*Yes, Damien. Take her. She wants you.* The voice whispered through his mind, and a languid lust thickened his senses until he could no longer think, could only feel.

*Asmos.*

He knew it was the demon. Could feel him and, logically, he knew he was buried deep within the throes of the curse, and he needed to leave now, to get out before it was too late. But he couldn't. He didn't have the strength. He didn't have the power of will to resist her taste, her touch.

Her love.

He broke free from her kiss, and caught a fleeting breath. "I love you, Emma. I'm overwhelmed with it, and don't know what to do." There, he'd said it. The words were out, and his heart was lying right there upon his sleeve for her to do with what she will.

She smiled at him, so sweetly, as her eyes shimmered with tears. She opened her mouth to speak, but before she could utter the words, he pulled away and hurried out the door. Heaven help him, he loved her.

Too much to be able to save her.

# Chapter 14

Damien's mistake was settling on him like a thick coating of acid rain, burning and eating away at his conscience. How could he have been such a clod? He was no longer a randy pup. There was no excuse for him not being able to physically control himself around Emma tonight. He'd come too close to succumbing to his rampant lust, and where would that have left Emma?

He knew better, and there was only one thing that could be done now. He'd have to destroy everything she felt for him. He'd have to tell her the truth. He had been foolish to think that by allowing things to progress this far, perhaps she wouldn't despise him once she discovered the truth. The sad thing was, she'd only despise him more. There was no pretending that the vampire blood within him didn't matter, when, in reality, it was all that mattered. It was who he was.

Restless, and knowing the worst was still ahead of him, Damien left the house, moving quickly through the estate's grounds, past the gardens in the back, the chipped fountain, the broken and overgrown hedges of what still held the faint outline of a traditional English maze.

He picked up the distinctive scent of the wolves, and could hear their padded footfalls as they followed his progress through the countryside. He wondered why they hadn't approached him.

He heard the soft murmurs of the vampires, and caught the scent of smoke. He slowed, cautiously approaching. He had a vague idea where they were camped, had sensed their presence the moment he'd stepped into the woods. Slowly, he approached the clearing. The clan of vampires had grown. He counted at least ten more than he'd seen the last time, and he couldn't help wondering why.

He stood behind a large tree, masking his presence, trying to determine what they were planning, why they were still here, even after they'd seen him and Emma drive away. Vampires, not social by nature, usually ran in small clans. Never had he seen one this large. Perhaps this was the congregation of more than one clan? If so, what did that mean? Were they all here for Asmos? For Emma?

The thought chilled him, and he wondered if the

Cadre or even P-Cell knew how many vampires were partaking in the "dark pleasure." Like an addiction, demon essence, once in the system, could be quite powerful.

Damien studied the vampires, and was just about to move to another spot to get a better look at the far side of the clearing when three young vampires hovering to his right moved, exposing something that made Damien's breath catch in his throat. He muffled an oath as disgust raged through him.

A woman, stripped naked, stood with her arms opened wide above her, each wrist was tethered to tree branches on either side of her, as were her feet. Her head hung down and masses of dark hair covered her face. Her creamy white skin was covered with shallow cuts and scratches. Worse, bite marks littered her body.

Every now and then, the girl would whimper and squirm. Her wrists and ankles were rubbed raw from pulling against the bindings. The distinct, heady metallic scent of blood rose on the air and filled him, and, to his horror, made his stomach churn with hunger.

A vampire walking past the girl, stopped, grabbed a fistful of her hair and pulled her head back. She cried as he pressed his lips against hers in a hard, demanding kiss. As he finished, he patted her butt and kept on walking, a hearty chuckle wafting in his wake. The woman looked after him, her red-rimmed eyes filled with terror.

Rage pumped through Damien's veins. His hands coiled at his sides, as frustration mounted within him.

Like cats, many vampires enjoyed playing with their victims, drawing out the kill until they became bored with them. Damien had heard the stories, but this was the first time he'd ever seen it up close and personal. There was nothing he could do about her right now.

Perhaps Nica, or even Dawn, was right. If Nicholai was a demon hunter, feeding off demon essence to make himself more powerful, and, in fact, enjoyed the torture and killing of humans, then he would have to be stopped. But would he be able to stop him? Would Damien be able to pull the P-Cell's vamp blaster's trigger, knowing it would obliterate his brother?

Damien pulled back out of sight of the clearing, realizing he had a choice to make, and it was one he could no longer run away from. If he was going to continue down this path and confront his brother, he would have to make a decision about how he was going to deal with him. It appeared Nicholai was the worst kind of vampire, he didn't just feed, he reveled in the kill.

Damien circled the camp, his finger caressing the vamp blaster in his jacket pocket, trying to convince himself, trying to work up the courage to do what needed to be done—exterminate his brother. The only family he had left, the last link to his past, to his humanity.

Unfortunately, Nicholai was stronger than Damien was. In order for Damien to succeed in taking him out, the attack would have to be quick, sudden and totally unexpected. He stayed to the outskirts, moving from one tree to the next, constantly watching the crowd, making note of which vampires were more powerful than others, how many there were, and who seemed to be aligned with who.

As he reached the far side of the clearing, a lone vampire stepped out from behind a large tree. "I've been waiting for you." A wide smile stretched across his heavily freckled ghost-white face.

Damien stilled. How was it he hadn't been able to shield himself from this vampire's senses? And if this Irish Joe with the shock of red hair had been able to sense him, how many others had? "Hope I didn't keep you long?" Damien said, rolling on the back of his heels to keep his stance deceptively casual.

"Not at all. We keep track of everything you do, Damien. Always have." The vampire stepped forward, waves of cocky assurance rolling off him.

"I'm surprised you've found my life that interesting." Damien reached with his senses, trying to determine if the pup was bluffing, but found he couldn't.

"You're not as elusive as you thought, eh?" the vampire challenged.

Damien took his measure, reading the subtleties in the energy pulses that surrounded him. He'd guess him at not more than a hundred and fifty years old. Not nearly old enough to match Damien's strength, and yet... He was obviously a blood drinker, and worse a demon feeder. Tests at the Cadre had shown increased strength and powers in vampires that partook of the "dark pleasure."

The vampire stepped closer. Damien dug in his heels, and readied himself for the fight. He considered the vamp blaster, but knew this model, one of P-Cell's first prototypes, only had one shot in it. That one he was saving for Nicholai. Instead, he wrapped his hand around one of the thin wooden stakes.

"Pretty little lady you've got back there at the house," the vampire said. "Almost as pretty as the last one you had."

Damien's heart beat hard against his rib cage. "What are you talking about?" he demanded.

"Oh, we have big plans for the pretty blonde. We're going to take our sweet time with that one. And maybe, just maybe, we'll let you watch." The vampire smiled, his mouth stretching, his fangs descending.

Damien's fingers flexed and tightened around the ash-wood stake, sharpened and honed to a fine point then dipped in silver. He took a deep breath and focused, staring not at the man's face, at the madness in his eyes, but at the target. Square in his chest. Without warning, Damien lunged.

With all the force, with all the pent-up anger and frustration he could gather, he drove the stake deep into the vampire's black heart and reveled in the moment the Irish vampire exploded into a plume of dust around him.

Damien stood back, wiped his hands on his pants, then replaced the stake in his pocket. He took a deep breath. That had been almost easy. Too easy.

He turned and faced his brother and ten of his cronies

standing behind him. Nicholai applauded, loudly. "Congratulations, brother. It appears there's a killer within you after all."

"I am nothing like you," Damien said with grit on his tongue.

Nicholai laughed. "You are me. You just choose not to see it." He stepped forward. "Come with us. Embrace your heritage. Embrace who you are. Stop trying to deny your inner self."

Damien's eyes narrowed. Self-help jargon from a demon sucker?

"Don't get all condescending with me. You're a killer. Same as us." Nicholai's arms gestured wide, encompassing the vampires around him. "You killed Kimmie, as easily as you killed this man, Vic. It's in your blood. It's who you are. That's why I can forgive you." The smile dropped and his eyes turned deadly. "Almost."

"Kimmie?" Damien asked, suddenly sure this wasn't going to end well.

"The redhead you attacked by your car."

"You've got that backwards, Nicholai, like so many other things. She attacked me."

"She was my wife."

Damien stared at him, his blood running cold.

Nicholai approached him, grabbed his shoulder and leaned in close. "My wife," he repeated.

Damien didn't know what to say, didn't know what he could say. Nicholai wrapped his arm around Damien's neck in a tight chokehold and walked forward toward his band of goons. "My brother has returned to us," Nicholai announced.

Unable to do much else, Damien walked with him, realizing with mild irritation that he really knew nothing about his brother, not even the type of man he'd become. Knowing it was most likely futile, he reached with his senses, trying to read his brother's intentions, but came up blank.

Nicholai looked at him, shook his head and chuckled. Apparently, his sensing abilities were working just fine. Damien didn't need special powers to read the intentions of Nicholai's clan, the waves of malevolence were almost overpowering.

They walked as a group back toward the clearing. The bonfire had been stoked and roared several feet above them. The heat rolling off it singed his face and burned his eyes. The rest of the clan were all standing at the outskirts of the clearing, feet wide, arms at the ready. Their gazes resting on Nicholai, as they awaited his command.

Damien's grip on the vamp blaster in his pocket tightened. He might get off a shot at his brother, but he'd never be able to take on all of them and survive. And he had to survive. If he didn't, there'd be no one left to protect Emma.

Surprise had been his only option, and now it was gone.

Emma refused to feel sorry for herself. Just because Damien had left her didn't mean she didn't matter to him. He was only being smarter than she. Protecting her from the Curse. But that didn't make his leaving hurt any less. Restless, she got out of bed. Pulling her robe tight against the chill, she walked toward the window and peered out into the night.

In the distance, she could see a large fire roaring. Fear seized her as she stared at it, trying to comprehend why there would be a fire that size in the middle of the forest. Quickly, she ran to Damien's room and knocked on the door. She waited, listening intently with her ear pressed to the door. She heard nothing.

"Damien?" she called softly and opened the door. The room was empty, the bed still made.

Damien! Suddenly, she was sure Damien was out there. Out by the fire. She ran down the back stairs, following the long hall toward the back of the house that Lucia used as her own.

*Hurry, Emma. Damien's hurt. He needs you.*

The words circled round Emma's mind as she pounded on Lucia's door, calling out her name, suddenly desperately afraid she'd been left in the house all alone. She flung open the door, just as Lucia spoke, her voice heavy with sleep. "What? What is it?"

Emma slumped against the door in relief. "Lucia, wake up. Damien's in trouble, I know it."

"Trouble?"

"Yes. He's gone. Now hurry." She ran toward her and flipped on the light next to the bed.

"Don't be silly," Lucia grumbled. "Why would Damien be in trouble?" She sat up, searching the rumpled bedcovers for her robe.

"Because he just is. There's a huge fire on the edge of the property. I saw it from my window. I don't know why, but I think Damien's out there. I think he needs us."

Lucia looked skeptical, and walked over to her window. "I don't see anything."

With frustration mounting, Emma rushed up behind her. "See." She pointed. "That orange outline over there? That's where it is. You'll have to go upstairs to see it clearly."

Lucia's forehead crinkled with lines of worry. "We must call for help from the village," she said, slipping her feet into her slippers and hurrying from the room. "The whole forest could catch on fire."

With Angel nipping at her heels and barking furiously, Emma chased after her. "That's fine, but then we have to go out there. We need to help Damien."

Lucia stopped in her tracks and spun round. "I am not going out there, and neither are you."

"Oh, yes I am." Emma bent down and scooped Angel up into her arms, shushing her. "Damien needs me. I feel it, and I'm not going to abandon him."

Lucia snorted. "Pooey."

"Lucia. I don't know if I have to tell you this, but there are vampires out there. Big, mean, ugly ones, and for all I know, they could be spicing Damien up for dinner right now."

Lucia only stared at her.

"I know it sounds crazy, but I saw them with my own eyes. And I—"

"You're not crazy," Lucia said softly. "I know."

Emma closed her eyes, thankful that she wasn't going crazy. That she wasn't in this alone. She stood up straight, squared her shoulders, and deepened her voice. "I can't let anything happen to him, Lucia. I love him, and I'm going after him, with or without you."

Lucia's eyes widened. "You can't. The Curse."

"I know. But we can't help it. We're in love. And see—" she gestured wide with her arms "—I'm still human. I haven't turned into some evil demon and killed everyone I know. You're perfectly safe with me."

Lucia muttered a few choice obscenities under her breath. "You've consummated?"

Emma's cheeks burned. "Not exactly."

Lucia shook her head, her lips pursed. "How can you love him? That's foolish talk. You don't know anything about him. He's not even—"

"I know enough to know he's kind, decent, thoughtful and all around a great guy," Emma interrupted. "And he makes me feel special."

Lucia rolled her eyes.

"Stop it," Emma demanded.

"Fine. But ask yourself, Emma. Would Damien want you running half-cocked out into the night right now? It is the night of the Equinox! Let's just make it through this night, then we'll worry about this great love next year!"

"I know. I understand what you're saying. And, no, he wouldn't want me out there. He wants me tucked up safe in bed sleeping. *Alone.* But that doesn't mean I'm going to sit idly by and do nothing as a clan of disgusting vampires feed off him."

Lucia threw up her arms in defeat. "Fine. Let me get dressed. You're not going anywhere without me, and you're certainly not going out into the deep, dark night unarmed. Is that clear?"

"Crystal," Emma said smiling. "I knew you'd come around."

"Don't push it, Emma."

Emma called after Lucia as she disappeared back into her rooms. "I'll never forget this. Not ever." She looked at Angel who was looking up at her with big brown eyes full of confusion. "No, you're not coming." She hurried down the hall and locked the dog up in the laundry room, just as Lucia came out of her rooms.

"Ready?" Emma asked.

"Not quite." Lucia hurried to open a door in the side of the stairwell and took out a large assortment of weapons.

Wide-eyed, Emma stared at them. "Should I guess that you've known about vampires for a while?"

"You could say that," Lucia muttered, and handed Emma a silver dagger and several stakes. "Know how to use them?"

Emma nodded. "Now I do."

The surprise in Lucia's eyes disappeared as she gathered up a crossbow and several ash arrows and entered the kitchen. "Are you sure you're ready for this?" Lucia asked, as they stood outside the cellar door.

Emma stared at the door, ignoring the nauseous turn of her stomach and nodded. "Ready as I'll ever be."

# Chapter 15

Nicholai pushed Damien into the clearing. Without hesitating, Damien strode toward the girl. She hung limply, obviously in distress from the heat. "This is why I'm nothing like you. Feeding on your victims is not enough for you, you must torture them, too."

Nicholai laughed. "Does she look tortured to you? She's just hanging there, while we admire her beauty, and she is beautiful, is she not?"

"Yes, beautiful and scared, with streams of tears running down her face." Damien grabbed one of her wrists, releasing her bonds. The woman clung to him with her free arm.

"Look in her eyes, dear brother. What do you see of our poor victim?"

Damien looked down into the young woman's eyes, and saw nothing but fear and hopelessness. He turned back to Nicholai with disgust on his face and anger in his heart. "She's only a scared girl, not much older than our sisters were the night they were slaughtered by a band of vampires no better than you."

In a move so fast Damien didn't see it coming, Nicholai had him pinned against a tree. Damien hung there, surprised by his brother's strength, his feet barely touching the ground. Nicholai leaned in close, his face mere inches from Damien's. "You've never tasted it?"

"Back off," Damien demanded, and pushed. Nicholai didn't budge.

"I knew you denied yourself the sweet drink but you've never once tasted human blood? You sit there staring down your nose at us in righteous indignation, and you've never once drunk the elixir that will complete you and make you who you are—a guardian of the night."

Damien laughed and shook his head. "A guardian? You delude yourself, brother. You're no guardian. You're a murderer, a fiend, the worse kind of monster."

Nicholai stood back, letting Damien's feet touch the ground. "You let those so-called protectors of mankind emasculate you. You might as well have given them your manhood."

"They have given me more than you could ever understand," Damien retorted.

"Really?" Nicholai challenged. "And that's why you're wandering aimlessly, without purpose, without hope. An empty shell?"

Damien couldn't respond. How could he? Nicholai was right. "You don't know what you're talking about," he defended, knowing the words sounded as lame as he felt.

Nicholai belted him hard across the face. "Tell me again how strong you are. Tell me how all your spiritual mumbo jumbo and working with crystals has made you stronger, has helped you discover your inner self."

Damien rubbed his jaw, then jumped to his feet and lunged. He got in two quick blows before landing with a thud face-down in the dirt. The vampires surrounding them roared with approval. In the midst of their raucous laughs and bellows ringing through the air, he heard a woman scream.

He looked up to see Nicholai scraping a long, sharp nail across the tender white skin of the woman's breast. Deep-red blood seeped from the cut and dripped down her chest. The sight of it, the smell of it filled his chest, burning down his throat, tensing his muscles. The woman's screams died down to choked whimpers. Nicholai retied her bonds.

Damien jumped to his feet, only to have Nicholai hit him again, this time square in the jaw. Rage surged through him and his fangs descended. If Nicholai wanted a fight, Damien would give him one. He squared his stance and kicked, landing a hard blow to Nicholai's stomach.

Nicholai grunted and bent over, but before Damien could go at him again, Nicholai had him on the ground at the woman's feet. He reached up and ran his index finger through the woman's blood, then shoved it into

Damien's mouth. It was only a taste, a drop, but it burned his tongue, his throat, his soul as anguish swept through him.

"You are one of us. You are a vampire. When you look into this whore's eyes, you should be able to see her sins." Nicholai pulled him up, dragging him up close to the woman. Horrified, Damien could only let him.

He couldn't fight back, nor could he understand the burning in his stomach, the wanting of more, the hunger that pierced him through and through. He wanted to, he *needed* to, he couldn't take his eyes off the trickle of blood dripping down the girl's creamy flesh. And when Nicholai pushed his face into her glorious breast, it was all he could do not to lap up every sweet drop.

As the sweet elixir ran down Damien's throat, he felt as if he'd been a man without food, without sustenance, and now he was fed. Fulfilled, in mind, body and spirit. Even the world around him changed, the colors sharpening and coming into clearer focus, his hearing intensified and so did his senses.

He could hear the woman's heart beating beneath her rib cage, could smell the delicate, intoxicating scent of her fear, could taste her soul in her blood.

"Now look into her eyes, dear brother," Nicholai said, grabbing Damien by the scruff of his neck and pulling him up to stare into the girl's eyes. What Damien saw horrified him.

"Just because they're human, brother, doesn't mean they're not evil. Doesn't mean they don't deserve to be part of the food chain. What separates us from the animals is that we can pick and choose which of them deserve to die, which of them *should* die."

Nicholai leaned close to the woman and took a small drink off her neck. Instead of screaming in pain, in fear, as Damien had expected, she swooned, her sweet nipples growing erect, the musky scent of her desire filling his nose. She whimpered and rubbed herself against him.

"She's my gift to you. Take a drink, Damien. Give the wench a moment of unending pleasure unlike any she's ever felt before she succumbs and dies."

Feeling his erection pushing at his pants, Damien wanted to do exactly as Nicholai said. He wanted to drink more of the sweet blood. Self-loathing filled him, and he turned and ran. Not because he was afraid, but because of the hunger, the drive, the need to grab that woman and sink his teeth into the soft skin of her neck was more than he could stand.

More than anything, he wanted to break into her flesh and suck deeply of her elixir. He wanted to hear her heartbeat thundering in time to his own, to drink from her until there was nothing left. He ran, because his unrelenting thirst and need scared him senseless.

He didn't get far before two of the goons stopped him, and dragged him back to the clearing, back to the girl. They brought him to her, and he couldn't control himself, he couldn't stop himself and he did what he had believed he never would, he fed, drinking as if he were just born and had no control over himself. He fed, devouring every last drop, hearing Nicholai's laughter and the rumble of rushing blood.

And when the woman's heartbeat slowed to a mere murmur he stopped, and fell to the ground, sick to the bottom of his soul.

"You're one of us now, brother," Nicholai mocked.

"This is crazy," Lucia grumbled as they passed the maze and moved into the forest. "We should go back to the house right now." The small flashlight wavered and bobbled, barely lighting the path before them.

"Damien needs us. I'm not going to leave him. Trust me, I can handle myself against a few vampires. I've been trained," Emma said, out of pure desperation.

Lucia snorted.

"Okay, so I'm full of it, what do you expect?" Emma admitted. "I'm as scared as you are, but I'm not going to leave him."

"Emma, he's Cadre. He's the professional. He knows what he's doing a whole lot more than we do."

"We're a team. We work together."

"You've known him for a few days! How can you even be sure he needs help?"

"I don't know," Emma admitted. "I just am."

Lucia looked back over her shoulder as they hurried through the trees, trying to keep to the narrow pathways. "Why haven't we seen those wolves?"

"Why are you complaining?"

"It's unusual. They're always hovering around."

"I don't know," Emma said, looking around her and biting her lip, "but count your blessings."

"Consider them counted."

They slowed and grew silent as they approached the clearing. From here, the bonfire was huge and, for a moment, Emma worried whoever had started it wouldn't be able to control it. What if it got out of hand? They could lose half the forest, not to mention Wolvesrain.

"I don't feel good about this," Lucia whispered, as they crept around bushes trying to get a closer look.

Emma had to admit that she didn't either. What if she were wrong? What if Damien was nowhere around here? What if she'd just led Lucia into a trap? How would she ever forgive herself? She stiffened her shoulders. These vampires wouldn't have stoked the fire so high unless they'd wanted it to be seen. The thought sent a chill coursing through her. She stepped closer, peering through the tall bushes, hoping she wasn't making a huge mistake.

"What do you see?" Lucia whispered, bumping into Emma's back as she tried to get a closer look.

"Nothing. Except a lot of people standing in a semi-circle around the bonfire." In greater numbers than she expected. An almost hysterical laugh bubbled up in her throat as the futility of the situation hit her. What made her think she could save Damien? Even if he was here? Even if he did need her help? "Do you think they're all vampires?" she whispered.

Lucia crossed herself. "We have to go back. Now."

Emma agreed. Lucia had been right. This wasn't just wrong, it was crazy. A fool's errand. She took one last glance over her shoulder as she turned away, then stopped. The crowd had parted, and she saw Damien bending before a young woman tied between two trees. His face had changed, his mouth stretched, his teeth extended into something vicious.

Unable to comprehend what she was seeing, Emma froze. Small sounds erupted from her throat as she tried to make sense of the deceit playing out before her. It had to be a lie, some awful game designed to confuse and trick her.

Unable to move, she stared at him, her eyes watering as she saw his teeth sharpen into fangs and pierce the girl's skin. Blood spurted, and Emma let out a soft cry as her knees weakened. Blackness circled the edge of her vision. Round and round her head spun, as nausea turned her stomach and the ground came up to meet her.

Vampires. *Not Damien.*

Her mind screamed. She retched and held herself. Lucia grabbed her around the waist and guided her away. "Hurry," she whispered, but Emma barely heard her. Bent over, they started running away from the clearing, moving as fast as they could away from the bonfire, away from the madness and back toward Wolvesrain.

Vampires were living right here, right in the forest behind her home. And they always had. Memories long-buried rose to the surface and assaulted her. They'd always been there, and she'd always known. She'd seen them before. When she was a child. In the cellar.

They'd come for her mother. They'd drunk from her,

until there was nothing left of her. They drained her mother, and left her there to die in Emma's lap. A primal guttural moan, starting deep in her stomach, rose out of her chest and filled the air.

"Shhh," Lucia demanded and hurried her even more, until they were practically running blind down the darkened path. The single beam of their flashlight bounced back and forth as they ran toward the safety of Wolvesrain, and away from the creatures who'd hurt her so much more than the wolves ever had.

Mental images assaulted her; all those memories she'd repressed for so long came flooding back. Just as Damien and the Cadre had wanted, and all she could think of was the blood.

So much blood. Everywhere.

A sharp pain pierced Emma's temples and burned behind her eyes as the fear and adrenaline pulsed and pounded. She remembered her mother holding her hand, squeezing it too tightly, pulling her toward her.

Just as Lucia was doing now, half pulling, half dragging her through the forest and toward the maze, toward the fountain filled with black water that emitted the stench of rot and decay. Back toward the cellar where it had all happened before, where her mother had looked down on her, a wicked smile playing across her face, and an evil glint in her eye. The vessel for Asmos.

Suddenly there was another man in the room. And he was smiling at her—his teeth sharp and pointed. They fought, the man and her mother, but the vampire won. He bit her mother, ripping open her neck. Her eyes widened, almost popping out of her head, as he sucked on her skin. And then the wolves attacked, and the man ran back the way he'd come, disappearing into the darkness.

Her mother's slackened mouth fell open, and her eyes fluttered closed. She moaned once or twice before falling to the floor. Emma held her head in her lap and brushed the hair back off her face. And that's when Mummy had made her promise never to fall in love. She'd pleaded with her, warning her of the Curse, and then all the life had gone out of her eyes and she stared up at the ceiling.

And Emma had begun to cry. And had never really stopped.

She swiped the tears off her face. A vampire had killed her mother. Not a wolf, not a pack of dogs and not a demon.

*A vampire.*


*Damien…*the voice whispered, like an insidious cold mist reaching deep within him to pluck his tightened nerves. He closed his eyes and sucked in a breath, trying to clear his mind. *Go after her, Damien. Save Emma.*

Emma? Here? He thought of her, and then he felt her. Felt her terror. Felt her flight. In gut-wrenching horror, Damien shook his head, clearing the blood-induced haze, the waves of pleasure undulating through his system. He looked up at the girl's lifeless form, and realized she was dead. And that he most likely had killed her.

He rolled over onto his knees and retched.

"Go after her," he heard Nicholai yell, and look up to see several of Nicholai's goons running toward Wolvesrain. He could hear Lucia's voice in the distance urging Emma forward, but worse, he could hear Emma, too. Her soft cries haunted him, and he knew they'd live forever in his heart.

"No," he yelled, pleading with his brother. "Let them go."

"Let them go?" Nicholai laughed. "What do you think all this was about, dear brother? You and your everlasting soul? You aren't that significant," he sneered. "It's about the girl. It's always been about the girl. You were just the bait. And you made it so pathetically easy." He winked and then turned and followed his men out of the clearing and toward Wolvesrain.

Toward Emma.

Damien got to his feet. He wavered unsteadily as the girl's blood rushed through his system. Two of Nicholai's cronies cut the ropes that held up the woman and threw her corpse into the fire. The smell of burning flesh sickened him, turning his stomach, until he retched again. His fists clenched with bottled-up rage and frustration.

All his life he'd trained, he'd studied, he'd worked to keep himself pure, and, in one short instant, Nicholai had taken all that from him. Now he was no better than the monsters standing in front of him laughing and pointing. Predators without souls, without hearts, without forethought or purpose. A perfect waste of life's precious gifts. All they knew how to do was prey, feed and kill.

Rage surged through him, flowing along his veins, milking his adrenaline, tightening his muscles, and sending a rush to his brain. With brutal precision he pounced, using the silver dagger in his pocket to destroy the two vampires in front of him. Even if they'd seen him coming, they wouldn't have stood a chance. As easily as they'd disposed of the girl, he picked them up and threw them into the flames.

He watched them burst into dust, and was surprised and horrified at the same time how good it felt. Like a dopamine rush, the pleasure, the thrill of the kill moved through him. He moved on and took more, fighting and killing as many of Nicholai's clan as he could. They would not take Emma. They would not take him. Not while he was still alive to do something about it.

His brother would pay for what he'd done to him. And for what he wanted to do to Emma. He approached a female, hiding in the bushes and, for a second, toyed with the idea of letting her go, of leaving her to fend for herself. But then he smelled the blood on her, the stench of death and deceit.

She would kill no more.

# Chapter 16

With Lucia a step ahead of her, Emma ran as fast as she could. Every part of her burned—her leg muscles, the bottoms of her feet, her lungs as she struggled to draw in enough air. She could hear their pursuers moving quickly through the bushes behind them, as the crush of footsteps reverberated around her. Terror gripped her, but she had to look back. She had to know.

She took a deep breath, and without slowing a step, turned and looked behind her. Her pursuer wasn't more than two arms-lengths behind her. And he wasn't alone.

She gasped, and tried to increase her speed, but her legs, already feeling like rubber, tripped over a tree root, sticking up out of the ground. She stumbled, regained her footing, and carried on just as an errant branch scraped across her face.

Hot tears of fear, of heartache blurred her vision. After all this, after all these years, she was going to die, not because she'd had a taste of love, or because demon wolves had ripped her to shreds, but because of a vampire. A monster who wanted the demon essence in her blood.

The maze, the house loomed ahead. She felt something brush her shoulder. She bent forward, willing her legs to carry her faster. If she could just make it to the maze, to the fountain, she would be all right. Didn't vampires need an invitation to enter her home? Or was that a myth? How could she not know? Why hadn't the Cadre, why hadn't Damien, prepared her for vampires?

Damien. Just the thought of him sent a burning, twisting pain through her heart. Because he was a vampire. And for all she knew, he wanted the essence in her blood, too. She pushed the thought out of her mind. She had to focus.

*Focus on me. On my voice. My touch.*

"Damn you, Damien," she muttered, and grasped one of the wooden stakes Lucia had given her just as the vampire behind her gained a hold on her shoulder and yanked her backward. Lucia cried out.

Emma hit the ground, hard. The air whooshed out of her chest. The vampire pounced on top of her, right onto the stake she was holding upright. He looked down at her, his eyes filled with feral hatred that widened into surprise before he burst into a shower of dust.

"Oh, my God, Emma," Lucia screamed. She ran back and pulled Emma up off the ground. "Keep going," she said, and turned to look behind them at the seven or eight vampires in heavy pursuit.

"We'll never escape them," Emma cried, as the futility of the situation hit her.

"Yes, we will. We need to get back in the house. Hurry."

Emma ran, following her. She could see the maze now, but as they approached it, the wolves stepped out from behind the overgrown hedges, one by one. Emma gasped and pulled Lucia to a stop. The two women clung to each other.

"Now what should we do?" Emma looked toward the kitchen door at the back of the house. Close enough to see and yet still so far. Huddling next to one another, they stepped, slowly and carefully toward that door, knowing they would never make it once the wolves decided to attack.

Behind them, the vampires stopped as they saw the wolves. They looked at one another, at Emma, then back at the wolves. "Vampires behind us, demon wolves in front. Thank God your father isn't here to see this," Lucia muttered.

Hysterical laughter bubbled in Emma's throat. There truly was nowhere for them to go, no way to escape.

"Emma, I'm here to help you," one of the vampires behind her said. "Now turn around and walk slowly and very carefully toward me. Don't make any sudden movements."

Emma turned and looked at the vampire who

promised rescue with his golden voice and slippery tongue. He held out his hand to her and stepped forward in front of the others. She knew his face, his obsidian eyes peering at her under sharp black brows, and it made her stomach turn. She took a quick step back, clutching Lucia as the wolves growled.

"Ah, so you remember me," he said, with a hint of amusement in his voice.

And she did. She remembered those eyes, the way they stared at her as he had sucked on her mother's neck, drinking her life force, then throwing her away, as if she were nothing more than a used paper cup. He'd taken her mother from her, her childhood, her peace of mind.

With the tenacity of a clinging vine, rage moved through her system, consuming her, replacing the fear, filling her with strength and purpose. She would not be this monster's victim any longer.

She pulled away from Lucia and tightened her hand around the silver dagger in her pocket. "I do remember you. You will not have me as easily as you had my mother."

Lucia gasped.

"Lucia, get into the maze or the house. Anywhere but here."

"I won't leave you."

Emma didn't have to turn back to see the determination written all over Lucia's face. She could hear it in her voice. And she knew, win or lose, she wouldn't have to fight this battle alone.

For a second, she allowed Damien's face, his voice, to enter her thoughts, but she pushed him away. She would not think of him. She had believed in him, she'd given him her heart, but he'd lied, leading her to believe they had a chance. A future. And he wasn't even human.

From now on he was dead to her. The conviction in her heart fueled the fury moving through her and hardened any lingering feelings she might have had left for him. She would do this without him.

"You have nowhere to run, darling. You might as well face the inevitable." The man, beast, whatever he was, stepped forward, his handsome face breaking into a wide smile.

Emma took a quick step back and bumped right into Lucia.

"I've got your back," Lucia said, and Emma could see her loading up the crossbow.

Hoping to block Lucia from the vampires and keep their attention focused on herself, Emma asked, "What have you done to Damien?"

"I've helped my brother see his true nature."

"Brother?" Emma asked, confused. Looking closely, she could see the resemblance in their stature and color. In the commanding way they both had of looking at her, in the cocksure confidence that they would succeed at anything they attempted, and in the annoying way they had of thinking they knew what would be best for her.

They didn't know, and this time they wouldn't succeed.

"Don't listen to him," Lucia spoke harshly behind

her. "He's trying to weaken and confuse you." She pulled pack on the crossbow's strings and let the arrow fly. Emma held her breath as the wooden arrow drove straight toward Damien's brother.

Feverishly, she hoped it would pierce his evil heart, but somehow he saw it coming, and ducked. The vampire directly behind him disappeared in a plume of dust.

"Now, that wasn't nice," the vampire said. "And here we were, just having a friendly chat."

"You come any closer, and you will all die," Emma threatened, mustering as much bravado as she dared.

The vampire laughed. "You are a spitfire. I can certainly see why Damien is so fond of you."

His words sliced through her heart, and left a burning ache in her chest.

"Ignore him," Lucia hissed over her shoulder and let loose another special arrow. This time it only grazed an arm.

"You ladies are starting to wear on my patience," the vampire said, losing his smile.

"We beg your pardon," Emma said, and flashed him a smile of her own.

"Kill the old one, but bring Miss McGovern to me. Untouched," the vampire ordered, then moved to the side, as his band of fiends charged.

Before Emma could so much as utter a gasp, she heard a ruckus behind her, turned, and saw the wolves charging her way. Her eyes widened as fear rushed through her veins, leaving her incapable of taking even the smallest step. Lucia yanked her backward, and within seconds the wolves were on them—and past them.

They rushed by, their legs moving in choreographed harmony, their nostrils flaring, their fangs bared as they pounced on the vampires. Emma stood shocked, her mouth hanging open, as the wolves ripped through the flock of bloodsuckers.

"What's happening?" she yelled.

"I don't know, but get ready," Lucia warned as several vampires ran past the wolf blockade, escaping their vicious fangs, and charged toward them.

Lucia sent more arrows flying through the air as she rushed backward toward the maze. Emma stood her ground, and using the techniques Damien had taught her at St. Yve, was able to hold her own, to fight, to defend.

As she fought off the vampires, she couldn't help thinking of Damien, but every time she did, she saw the blood, the fangs. That poor dead girl, hanging naked and covered in bite marks.

*My brother.*

Damien was a vampire. He'd always been a vampire. That's why the Cadre thought he would be the best agent to help her with Asmos and his wolves. Why hadn't he told her? Why let her bare her heart for him, her soul? He'd known what was happening, and still he'd let her fall in love with him.

Anger set a blaze to the pain in her heart. And with the fury came the power. And with the power came the strength. One by one, Emma annihilated any vampire that came near her, and with each kill, she grew more certain that she would win. She had the power to triumph over evil. No longer would she live in fear of the wolves, of demons, or even vampires. Now, they would live in fear of her.

With the conviction of her thoughts, power surged through her. And she liked it. Liked the control it gave her, the courage, the confidence of knowing that from now on, she could take care of herself. She didn't need anyone, certainly not Damien the vampire.

In the clearing, Damien fought, killing one vampire after another. It wasn't too difficult, since it appeared the higher echelon of the vampire clans, along with Nicholai, had gone after Emma. He heard her scream, and his blood ran cold. All he could do now was hope that they wouldn't kill her before he had a chance to get there.

Rage filled his veins and made it easy to do what needed to be done, to do what the Cadre never would have agreed to—one by one, massacre what was left of Nicholai's clan. He hated to admit it, but it felt good. He felt as though he was accomplishing something, even though most were fledglings, scavengers who fed off what was left of the warrior's pickings. They disgusted him.

But as he looked around the clearing, *he* disgusted himself. There wasn't one vampire left. He melted into the bushes, moving quickly, heading for Wolvesrain, for

Emma. As he reached the edge of the estate, what he saw made him stop in his tracks. Lucia and Emma fighting off two or three vampires and holding their own.

Even more surprising were the wolves, ripping and tearing into vampire flesh, biting and gnawing until the vampires pleaded, screaming for death. They appeared to be fighting as a team, Emma and her legion of demon wolves. The scene was so much like what had happened before, back on the night that he'd been reborn, that all he could do was stare in dumbstruck horror.

He recalled the tormented screams of his gypsy clan, of his sisters, as Asmos, in the body of Camilla, had decimated his people. And if Asmos hadn't been bad enough, the vampires came, wanting in on the action. His maker, Nicholai's maker, had wanted Asmos's essence. The rest of his clan just wanted blood.

Remembering that night and the carnage they'd left behind was the reason he'd become who he was and joined the Cadre. He believed in the Cadre's philosophy and what they did. And sometimes, as now, trapping and ridding the world of evil demons and bloodthirsty vampires was a worthy endeavor.

But sometimes the Cadre's rules left the hunters vulnerable, and the cost became too high to pay. This was one of those times. The Cadre would not be receiving any specimens for study and interrogation this time. In fact, they'd never receive anything from him again. His days with the Cadre were over. It was too late for him, he had too much blood on his hands. Too much blood within him.

His heart, saturated with human blood, was no longer pure. Never again would he be able to resist the bloodlust flowing through his veins. In fact, he was certain he no longer had the strength necessary to pull Asmos or any other demon into the containment crystal. He was too tainted. Too far gone.

And because of his weakness, Emma would pay the price. *Emma.* He looked at her, rocked once again by the overwhelming feeling of déjà vu. Only this time it wasn't Camilla fighting against the vampires, it was Emma.

A shudder moved through him. Asmos. The demon was already working his insidious magic. Already calling to her, tempting her, lying to her. Making her feel powerful, making her believe she could trust in him, that he was her answer, that he was the one who could give her what she needed.

Unable to tear his gaze from her, he watched, sickened, as she bent to embrace the wolves, smiling as she rubbed her face into the soft, thick fur around their necks. His fault. All his fault. He'd let her down. His lies and betrayal had given Asmos the way in, the foothold he needed.

So, consumed with guilt and remorse, Damien didn't see the last warrior coming. Didn't noticed as the warrior raised the club high above him. He sensed him, though, and, at the last minute, looked up as the club came crashing down to shatter against his skull.

Damien's knees gave out and he dropped to the ground, his world turning black as the sound of Emma's screams ricocheted through his mind.

# Chapter 17

Emma looked up in horror as the vampire brought the club down upon Damien's head. He dropped instantly, heavily, to the ground. She screamed and scrambled to her feet. Before the vampire could club him again, an arrow whizzed through the air past Emma and straight into the vampire's evil heart.

Emma raced toward Damien with the wolves following close behind. They positioned themselves protectively around Emma and Damien, each facing outward as if they were keeping watch. As she looked at them, she wondered again why they were helping her.

Why, after all these years when she had lived in fear of them, were they suddenly there for her? Perhaps it wasn't the wolves she'd needed to be afraid of, but the vampires. Perhaps that's why they'd come back again and again, year after year, to protect her from the vampire who'd killed her mother.

Damien's brother.

Her heart broke with the thought. Was Damien in on this horrible plan with his brother all along? Had he meant her to fall in love with him? She'd been lured out of the house and into the vampires' trap by her certainty that Damien was in trouble. That he needed her. Had she been right? Had he needed her? Had she arrived too late?

She lifted his head onto her lap and stared down at him, brushing the hair back from his forehead, the same way she had done for her mother on that dreadful night so long ago. The side of Damien's head was covered in blood. A deep gash split his skin where the club had hit him.

"We should get him back to the house," Lucia muttered, staring over her shoulder at the wound.

"How do you know we can trust him?"

"Because of you."

"What?" Emma looked up at her in confusion. "What's that supposed to mean?"

"When you saw that vampire attack him, you reacted with your heart, not your mind. You know in your heart you can trust him. That he means us no harm."

As Emma thought on Lucia's words, tears burned her eyes. Was Lucia right? Did she know in her heart that Damien's intentions were pure? Did he love her?

Or was she just a fool? Emma pushed the thoughts away. "It doesn't matter. We can't take him back to the house anyway. He's too heavy. Besides, you might be sure I can trust him, but I'm not."

"Well, we just can't leave him here," Lucia protested. "He's part of the Cadre. They sent him here to help us."

Emma almost laughed out loud. "Since when do you trust or even care about the Cadre?"

Lucia's lips thinned into a straight line. "I'm not always right all the time, you know." She took a step back and looked around them. "There don't seem to be any vampires left."

"Sounds too good to be true," Emma muttered.

"I'm going to go get some ice and towels. Will you be all right here?"

Emma nodded. "I'll stay. I have the wolves." She looked at the four animals keeping guard around them and smiled as a feeling of warmth stole over her. Suddenly she knew the wolves would always be there for her, would protect her and take care of her. She was no longer alone.

Damien stirred. She took his hand in hers. There was blood under his nails, and she couldn't help wondering if it was his or the young woman's. How could she have been so close to him and have missed all the signs? He wasn't human, and she hadn't even noticed.

She ran her finger across his lips, remembering the way they'd felt against hers, remembering the soft, loving caress of his tongue, and her heart ached for him, for the dreams she'd had. His eyes opened and he stared at her, his blue gaze drawing her in, pulling her to him.

"Emma?" he whispered.

She tried to give him a reassuring smile, but just couldn't seem to make her lips move. "You're going to be all right," she whispered over the large lump in her throat.

He winced and tried to sit up, but fell back against her. "Where's Nicholai?"

She looked around her. One of the wolves whined at the name. "There's no one here. I think—I hope— they're all dead. In any case, no one will be bothering us now. Not anymore. Not with my wolves here."

He winced. "He's dangerous."

"Your brother?"

"Yes." He sat up, and cradled his head in his hands.

"So, how long have you been a vampire?" she asked casually, as if she were asking if he wanted milk and sugar with his tea.

"I know I should have told you," he whispered.

Her eyes narrowed. "Damn right." She didn't bother trying to hide her rage, her fury at his lies.

"Nica warned me. I just didn't…"

"Didn't what?" she asked, as her patience quickly fled.

He looked up at her. "Didn't want you looking at me the way you're looking at me now."

"And how is that?" she asked, but she knew. She could only imagine. "With disgust, revulsion? Absolute to-the-core hatred?"

"You don't really feel that way," he said, and leaned

in close to her. "I know how you feel about me. How you really feel."

Her heart quickened at his nearness while her jaw stiffened. "It was a lie. Everything between us has all been lies, from the very beginning."

He hung his head, his shoulders slumping, and, for a moment, for the teeniest, tiniest second, something akin to pity moved through her. She had cared once. A lot. She didn't want to hate him. But she did.

"I remembered something tonight," she said.

"Yes?" He looked up at her, and the raw emotion in his eyes bored through her defenses. She stiffened her resolve.

"Your brother. I've seen him before."

Concern and something akin to fear filled his expression. "When?"

"The night my mother died. He fed off her. He killed her."

Damien stared at her for a moment, his gaze hard as he processed the information.

"I saw him. I was there. He…" Her voice cracked. "He smiled at me."

"I'm sorry." He moved to touch her, to offer comfort, but she wasn't interested in his comfort, in anything he had to offer.

He took a deep breath, and tried to capture her gaze, but she wouldn't let him. "My brother—" he began "—like our maker, feeds off demon essence, for the rush, the power."

"So he hunts down innocent people and kills them,

just because they're unfortunate enough to have a demon's essence within them? That's disgusting."

"I suppose, but that's the way things are. Some vampires feed off the weak, some the mentally deranged and the criminally inclined. Some prefer demons."

"And you?"

"I drink animal blood. Before tonight, I had never touched human blood."

She stared at him, searching his face, his eyes, probing for the lies, the deceit, the path he was trying to dig back under her defenses and back into her heart. "What happened tonight?" she asked, with a shaky voice. Knowing the moment the question was out that she'd given him a way back in.

"Nicholai was determined to tear me down. And he knew just the way to do it."

"And you couldn't refuse? You couldn't stop him? That girl is dead."

"Trust me, there was nothing I could do." The dejection in his voice, the raw pain emanating from him, did more than his words ever could do to convince her he spoke the truth. And, for a moment, she almost felt sorry for him.

Almost.

"I'm sorry, Emma. I've failed you."

She choked. "Excuse me?"

"I won't be able to help you now. With Asmos. We need to call Nica. We need reinforcements. I'm no longer pure, no longer strong enough to pull him out of the wolves and into the stones."

She stared at him confused. "Just because of a bump on the head? Don't you vampires live forever?"

He smiled. Weakly, but it was there, and damn him if it didn't cause the smallest whisper of a flutter inside her battered heart.

"It's because of the woman's blood. It's weakened my resolve. It's made me more susceptible to evil."

"Perhaps, but it seems to me if you've been able to resist the bloodlust all these years, then you should be able to resist the call to evil."

He stared at her, contemplating her words.

"In any case, I'm stronger now. Stronger than I've ever been before. Together we can still fight Asmos. If need be."

"No, we can't."

A surge of anger fired up inside her again. "Stop being such a defeatist! Stop telling me what I can and cannot do."

She had to clamp down just to keep from shrieking at him.

"It's Asmos's essence that's giving you the strength, the rush that makes you feel all-powerful. It's what Nicholai wants from you. It's the same feeling he gets after drinking the essence. Asmos is growing stronger within you, even without you fulfilling the curse, he's filling you, feeding off your rage, transforming you. I'm worried…if you let him, if you succumb, he could take you over completely."

"That's absurd," she countered. But even as he said the words, a trickle of fear seeped into mind, expanding and growing until she felt consumed with it.

"Is it? Think about it, Emma. You referred to the wolves as yours."

"What?" she said, her voice barely louder than a whisper.

"You said 'my wolves.'"

"Did I?" She tried to think back, but couldn't remember. Was he right? Had she thought of them as hers? She looked at the animals and again felt warmth and peace steal into her heart. She pushed out Damien's words, his negativity. He just didn't understand.

"Emma, close your eyes. Practice the breathing I taught you. Look inward and tell me what you see."

"I can't." She didn't want to. She didn't want to fall for any more of his tricks. His lies. She liked the way she felt right now—in charge, in control.

"You can."

Of course, she could. But why should she? He was bringing back the fear. She could feel it encroaching, pushing on the borders in her mind. It was growing, permeating her blood vessels, tightening her muscles and constricting her lungs until suddenly she wasn't sure she could breathe.

Damien took her hands in his. "It's okay. Just focus on my voice, on my touch. On me. Push it out, Emma. The darkness, the fear. Imagine the light. Bright, white light. Pull it in, until it chases the darkness away, so there isn't a corner left it can hide in. You can do it, you have the power."

Yes, she had the power. Her breathing evened and she did as he said, pulling in the light, riding the light, feeling it as it pervaded every part of her, until suddenly she could breathe again, and she wasn't so angry, or so scared.

She opened her eyes and looked down at her hands clutched in Damien's. She looked deep into his blue eyes, and felt tears well in her throat. "Thank you," she whispered, and let her forehead rest against his.

"Are you okay?"

She nodded. "I am now."

"Come on, let's go in."

The wolves whined as they stood. Damien watched them nervously, but they didn't follow as they walked toward the kitchen door.

Lucia was waiting for them with towels and ice. Damien took them from her. Emma almost seemed her old self again as she scooped her little dog up into her arms and covered its face with kisses. Damien couldn't help smiling and feeling a little sad at what they'd had, and what they'd now lost.

He wouldn't dwell on it, not tonight. He was exhausted, and wanted nothing more than to rejuvenate. It had been too long since he'd slept, and he knew the pain, the emptiness of his life would catch up with him soon enough.

Probably as soon as he walked out Wolvesrain's front door.

It looked as if the old Earl of Wolvesrain would get the last laugh after all. He took out his cell and called Nica, and filled her in on the night's activities. Well, not everything. There were some things she and the Cadre were better off not knowing. For his own safety. The last thing he wanted was to be entombed under St. Yve.

"The night of the Equinox is almost over. Emma has made a truce of sorts with the wolves and with Asmos. I don't foresee any more problems. At least not this year."

"How can you be sure?" Nica asked.

"It's just been a long night. A lot has happened. Asmos came, he left, the party's over."

"And your brother?"

"I'm afraid most of his clan had to be terminated."

"There was no other way?"

"I'm sorry. We did the best we could, but we were terribly outnumbered. I completely understand if this means I will no longer be able to be of service to the Cadre. Or be welcomed at St. Yve. I've made my peace with that." In fact, he was more than at peace with it. If he didn't lay eyes on St. Yve for another millennium, it would be soon enough.

"You did what you had to do, Damien. There are some of us here who believe that, who believe in you."

Her words twisted in his gut. "I appreciate that." And he did, he just wasn't quite sure he believed it.

"You didn't mention what had happened to Nicholai," Nica pressed.

"I can't be sure. I doubt we got rid of him that easily, but I haven't been able to sense him anywhere around here."

"Well, let's hope he's gone for good."

"I wouldn't count on it," Damien muttered, and planned on spending a few more weeks in his flat in the village just to be certain Emma was safe.

"And the Curse?"

"I believe we're good for now. Asmos and his wolves appear to have gone back to whatever demon dimension they hail from. I can't sense them around either. We'll just have to wait and see if they come back again next year."

"Thank you, Damien. For everything. Tell Emma we'll be sending her father home in a fortnight. He has made a remarkable recovery."

"I will. She'll be pleased to hear it."

Her voice softened. "Take care of yourself, Damien."

"Always." He disconnected the line. Only a few more hours left until daylight. He kissed Lucia on the cheek. And Emma, his lips trembling as a slight tremor went through his system. He would miss her sweet smile, and the way she used to look at him with those beautiful, shining cornflower-blue eyes.

But she was no longer interested in making time with monsters. He could read it in the way she stiffened as his lips touched her skin, and the guarded look she gave him.

He turned, and went up the stairs to his room, closed the curtains, and searched for any sign of his brother and the wolves one last time before he moved the armoire into place in front of the window.

All was clear.

It was finally over.

He lay on the bed, closed his eyes and fell instantly
to sleep. The last images flitting across his mind were
fields of heather swaying beneath a cornflower-blue
sky.

## Chapter 18

Emma watched Damien climb the stairs, his shoulders slumped but his head held high. She'd heard his conversation with Nica. Now that Asmos and Damien's brother were no longer a threat, he would be leaving soon. Maybe even before she woke, and chances were she'd never see him again. He'd disappear back into the darkness from which he'd come and become nothing more than a shadow on her memory.

A blip of happiness in a lonely life. Sadness filled her for what could have been. If only…she turned away.

"Go after him," Lucia said, softly.

"No," Emma responded, fighting back the tears. It was better this way.

"You can't run from love. Just because he'll be gone, doesn't mean you'll stop loving him. That you won't think about him every day and wonder if perhaps you'd made a mistake. Don't live your life in regret, Emma. Go talk to him. Be certain before you let him go."

She knew Lucia was right, but that didn't make it any easier. Some things were better not faced. And the fact that he was a vampire was a big one. "What about the Curse, Lucia? Weren't you always warning me against love? Why the sudden change?"

"Because I want you to be happy. You can't live the rest of your life rambling around this big old house with me. And besides, you heard what Damien said on the phone. Asmos and his wolves are gone for now. Next year, I'll worry."

Emma looked around the kitchen. Was Lucia right? Would the two of them still be standing here in another twenty or thirty years talking about this night, talking about what could have been? A shudder moved through her.

How would she feel if she never saw Damien again? Did she still love him, even after what she'd seen? Even though she knew the truth about him? And even if she did, how could they possibly make it work?

"You know," Lucia said, while pulling a container of butter pecan ice cream out of the freezer. "Sometimes these things get a little messy. There aren't always easy answers to life's big questions. Sometimes you just have to follow your heart." She opened the cabinet and reached for a bowl. "Want some?"

Emma shook her head. "No, thanks." She thought of what Lucia had said, and tried to listen to her heart, but she just wasn't sure how she felt any more. She wished Damien were here with them, sharing a bowl of ice cream. Maybe then she'd know whether or not his mere presence could still make her heart skip a beat. Or if he still caused that strange flutter in her stomach when he looked at her, or if he could still make her feel beautiful.

She sighed. "I'm going to bed. I'll see you in the morning. Maybe by then I'll know what to do."

"Sounds like a plan to me," Lucia said, and smiled as she savored a bite of sweetness.

Emma climbed the stairs to her room, dropped Angel on her bed, then turned toward Damien's room, her feet feeling like lead as she walked down the hall. Would he want to see her? Did he still care? She knocked softly on the door and, for a second, feared he wouldn't be in there. That she'd open the door and he'd already be gone, and her chance would be lost.

How would she feel if she never saw him again? Pain constricted her heart at the thought. She raised her hand to knock again when the door swung open. Damien stood before her, hair rumpled, dark shadows under his eyes.

"I'm sorry to bother you."

He stared at her, no smile, no warmth in his gaze, just the darkness of defeat. An awkward silence hung between them.

"I was afraid you'd leave and I'd never see you again."

A shadow passed before his eyes, and she knew that was exactly what he'd been planning.

"We need to talk. I need you to promise me that you won't disappear before we have a chance to work this out, to determine how we really feel for one another."

"I can't do that," he said softly, with no emotion in his eyes or his voice.

Fear clutched her heart. "Damien—"

"Look Emma, I'm tired. I can't do this right now."

"Then later?" she asked, her voice rising.

He nodded, and shut the door.

But he hadn't promised. And as she stood there, she knew there wouldn't be a later. If she didn't do something about this, about him now, she'd lose him forever. And forever was just too long a time to live alone, to live without love.

She ran back down the hall to her room, a plan already forming in her mind.


As Emma showered and changed into something soft and slinky, she wondered if she was doing the right thing. Did she really want to take this step? Was she making a mistake falling in love with a vampire? A monster?

She brushed out her long hair, then stopped and looked at her face. Really looked, and this time she saw what Damien saw—a beautiful woman with a few ugly scars. They were a part of her, but they didn't make up who she was. He had showed her that. He saw past the scars to the woman within. Would a monster do that?

She thought of Nicholai and knew there was no comparison. *He* was the monster. *He* was the one who'd given up his soul in his quest for power, not Damien. Nicholai was the one who enjoyed human suffering, who had no more heart and compassion than a psychopath.

She took one last look, assuring herself that this was what she wanted, then crept back down the hall to Damien's room. Quietly, she cracked the door open. For a moment, as she stepped into the darkness, she feared he'd left. But then she heard his deep rhythmic breathing and knew she wasn't too late. She still had a chance to prove to him that they belonged together. That together, they could fight anything.

Hadn't he been the one to tell her that?

She lit the candle on the bedside table, and waited for him to stir. As she watched the light flicker across his handsome face, she knew she didn't want him to leave. He'd warned her not to fall in love with him, but she'd done it anyway. Now here she was, for better or worse, in love with a vampire.

She shook her head and sat on the side of the bed. She wasn't even sure what that meant. What did she know about vampires? All she knew was that she couldn't let him walk out her door without him knowing the truth about how she felt for him. She couldn't take the chance that he'd leave and she'd never see him again. She couldn't spend the rest of her life alone at Wolvesrain. Especially not now that she'd had a taste of love. Of happiness. She couldn't let him leave her, at least not until she'd had a chance to show him how much he meant to her.

Making her decision, she pulled up the covers and slipped into the bed next to him. He stirred gently but didn't wake, so she kissed him, softly at first, then deeper, brushing her tongue across his lips. They parted slightly and she slipped her tongue into his mouth, tasting him, moving her lips over his.

He moaned and pulled her to him, wrapping his arms around her and deepening the kiss. She smiled, even as he crushed his lips to hers, and stole her breath. Then his eyes opened and he pulled back, immediately releasing her.

"Emma?"

She smiled, and barely touched her lips to his. "Hello handsome."

"I thought—"

"I couldn't wait," she interrupted and rained kisses down his chin, his neck, gently pulling the skin in the hollow between his neck and collarbone into her mouth. "I know you said we'd talk tomorrow, but I don't want to talk. And I don't want to be alone. Not tonight." She ran her hand down his smooth chest, realizing he was naked. Her smile widened as her thoughts turned wicked.

She loved him. And she was ready to show him how much. Even if he left her in the morning, she wanted her first time to be with someone she loved, with someone she knew loved her back.

"Emma, this isn't right. We can't—" He didn't finish.

She kissed his smooth skin as she inched lower down his body. She pressed the palm of her hand against his heart and felt his heartbeat quicken. "It will be all right," she said, and ran her tongue lightly across his nipple, pleased when it jerked to attention. "I just want to show you how much you mean to me."

"Emma," he said roughly, and grabbed her arms.

She might have been alarmed by the intensity in his eyes, by the harshness of his tone, if she weren't feeling his long, hard erection through the thin satin of her nightgown. He wanted her, too.

"I'm not letting you leave me without a proper goodbye," she insisted, and shifted, rubbing herself suggestively across his erection, giving him no possible way to refuse her.

He inhaled a quick breath. "Are you trying to seduce me?"

The hint of incredibility in his tone had her smile widening. "Would that be so bad?"

"But you know the truth about me." His voice cracked as he said the words, and the pain hidden in the depths of his eyes made her heart ache.

"You're right. I know how special you are, and what's more, I know how you make me feel. I love you, Damien. And I want to share that love with you."

Damien wasn't sure what to do, how to respond. Every fiber in his being was telling him this was a mistake. It was all happening too fast, and things were quickly spiraling out of control. But with each light touch of her soft fingers and her sweet lips, the fire running through his veins grew hotter and hotter. She was becoming more and more difficult to ignore.

"I don't think this is such a good idea," he began, but lost his thought as she continued with her insistent kisses, and delicate touch. She pressed herself against him. Her nipples, hard little buds through the satin of her gown, rubbed erotically against the bare skin of his chest, making him stiffen with each lithe movement.

He moved his hand up and down the sweet curve of her hips, loving the feel of the smooth satin against his skin. Tentatively, he touched her breast with his thumb and forefinger, sliding his fingers down, encircling, teasing. She gasped a breath.

"Emma, you're very beautiful, very desirable, and I'm sure you can feel how much I want you right now, but this…this really isn't such a good idea. Not now. Not yet."

She brought her hand lightly over his as he continued to caress her breast. "You're right, Damien. I can feel how much you want me," she said, then she sat up, and to his astonishment, pulled that satin garment up over her head.

Except for her panties, she was naked, and with the glow of the flickering candlelight against her skin, utterly breathtaking. Blood roared through Damien's ears, and his breath quickened. She lay down next to him, with nothing to stop him from feeling her silky smoothness, or the heat of her desire. She was so beautiful, so perfect.

"It's okay, Damien. We can just lie here…and talk," she said, and ran her fingers lightly down his chest, his stomach, stopping just below his bellybutton. His erection jumped at the nearness of her touch. She looked at it and smiled.

He pulled her to him, crushing her tightly against him, her lips to his, her sweet breasts pressing hard against his chest. He kissed her deeply, tasting her innocence, her passion, her yearning.

She moaned slightly, and tried to push herself closer to him. He parted his legs, and she slipped between them, the weight of her pushing against his erection, making it throb with anticipation.

"Are you sure?" he asked, his voice breathy, as they broke from another kiss. He pushed the hair off her face so he could see her eyes, could look into her soul to make certain she knew what she was doing, and that she wouldn't regret it later.

"More than I've ever been sure of anything."

"I won't hurt you."

"I know."

But did she? Could she be so sure? He had to wonder—did she really trust him? Was she completely free of doubt? Or perhaps she really had no idea what being a vampire really meant, the kind of power he had.

To prove to himself whether or not she really trusted him, he ran his lips in a spring of kisses down the exquisite column of her throat, nipping gently, but being careful, not to break the skin. He'd never hurt her, but he had to know if she really trusted him. After everything that had happened, could she love him without that trust?

Now that he had human blood racing through his system, the transformation was complete. After more than two hundred and fifty years, he was truly a vampire. And he felt it in his blood, the power, the lust. The need for blood. Would he be able to fight that need? Would he be able to stop himself from biting even Emma? The one person he truly loved in this world?

He could have cried out with the horror of it. He could never, would never, hurt her. But how did he really know? Now that he'd drunk the elixir, could he really trust what he might or might not do?

Emma tensed under the ministrations of his tongue, as he moved it steadily back and forth down her neck and over the delicious lines of her collarbone. Was she tensing in fear, or passion?

He knew from the response of the girl tied to the tree how she would respond to his bite. The pure eroticism of his teeth piercing her skin, the metallic taste of blood on his tongue, no matter how slight, would be heaven for them both.

She would reach pinnacles of pleasure never before experienced. The joining of their bodies, physically, mentally, he'd feel what she felt, and it would be magnified a hundredfold for her.

He ran his hand across her full breasts, teasing her tight hard nipples, lightly pinching, pulling. She gasped, then let out a small moan and arched, pushing herself into his hand, squeezing those beautiful, soft thighs together.

And he knew what she was feeling, for he felt it, too. The exquisite pleasure building between her legs, longing for pressure, for him to take the small nub buried within her satin curls and do to it what he was doing to her breasts. But he wouldn't, not yet.

Instead he took her breast in his mouth, and suckled gently at first, reveling in the feel of her hands tangling in his long hair, in the soft fullness in his mouth.

"Damien, please," she pleaded. Oh, and he liked the sound of her pleading. But he wouldn't give her the release she was looking for, not yet.

"I can make you feel things you've never felt. I can make you scream for me. Do you want me, Emma?"

"Oh, yes. Yes."

"Do you trust me?"

"Yes. Yes."

"Are you sure?" He sat up and looked down into her face, into her beautiful blue eyes laden with desire, and searched for the truth. She grabbed him behind the neck and pulled him down to her. "Yes," she whispered, and thrust her tongue into his mouth.

Fire ran rampant through his system. He crushed his lips to hers, tasting her, demanding, devouring. She tasted sweet, trusting, innocent. Her innocence was almost overwhelming. He had to do it right, to be careful, or she'd sweep him along with her desire, and they'd both be lost.

Patting, stroking with his palm flat, he slid his hand

across her body, moving to her feet and rubbing the soft curves of her calves, running his tongue in the grooves behind her knees and up the insides of her thighs.

She whimpered, little mewling sounds of pleasure, and suddenly he believed what she believed, that he wasn't a monster. That he was a man who could make her happy, who could love and protect her for a lifetime.

"You mean so much more to me than I can show you physically. I could never touch you gently enough, or make you feel enough passion to describe how I feel," he said, his voice husky as he spoke the words.

Her body trembled beneath him. He slid both hands up her hips, caressing every inch of her, with his fingers, his tongue, his lips.

Emma couldn't catch her breath. Her mind went blank as Damien touched her, as he pressed his body against hers. He was long and hard, sliding against her, his need rampant and intoxicating. She squeezed her legs together as overwhelming sensations swamped her body, blocking out all thoughts but the feel of his touch as he stroked her backside, his fingers moving under the edge of her panties.

"Yes," she breathed, her voice raw. "Take them off."

His touch was magic; his deft fingers stroked and probed places that had never been touched before. Lost in the arousing sensations, she found herself almost desperate for something she didn't understand but had to have. His touch, his kiss, him, inside her.

He continued his teasing as he gently opened her legs.

Her body tensed, tightening with such need she thought she might explode. She grabbed him closer, shifting until she felt the tip of him moving against her. She wasn't afraid, in fact, she welcomed it. She wanted it, more than she'd ever wanted anything in her life.

As he nestled between her legs, she spread them wider, then grabbed his buttocks and pulled him to her. In one quick movement, he was where she wanted him. He was hot and hard, the pain was quick and brutal, and then it was gone.

He moved slowly at first, giving her body time to adjust, to expand around him. Like butter cleaved by a hot knife, she melted, surrounding him with her warmth.

She lifted her hips, matching his rhythm, letting the passion build once more. It expanded within her, hot and languid, filling every part of her mind, her body, her soul. As they moved, two bodies joining and becoming one, she was pushed closer to that unknown edge, and he was all she had to hold on to.

She grasped his hands, her fingers intertwining with his, as he moved faster, harder, pushing deeper and deeper. She rocked, canting her hips. Her breath came in quick gasps, unable to stay more than a second in her chest.

"Please," she begged. Wanting some sort of release from this sweet torment. Needing it to stop, yet not wanting it to at the same time. Wanting the pleasure to go on and on always.

"Damien," she whispered his name, and the sound

of it felt wondrous to her ears. His tongue filled her mouth, and she tasted him, and knew she could not go another day without his taste, his smell, his touch.

"I love you. Please, don't leave me." There she'd said it. She'd laid her heart there on her sleeve, and she hoped he would take it.

"I won't. I promise. I couldn't."

She was getting closer, rising higher.

"You mean everything to me," he said. "You've given me back a reason for being. I love you."

Tears filled her eyes at his words. Then, as she moved closer and closer to that unknown edge, she grabbed his arms, tilted her head back and screamed. And just before she plummeted over, she heard something, softly at first, then louder.

Laughter. And the howling of wolves.

# Chapter 19

The laughter grew louder and louder in Emma's mind, and with it came the thick, inky blackness filling her as if she'd slipped into a pool of cold, liquid tar. The sludge moved slowly through her system, leaving a trail of fear in its wake.

In a far-off distance, she could hear Damien's voice. She reached for him, but couldn't seem to find him. She opened her mouth to speak, but her tongue was too thick, too heavy to move.

*Asmos.*

With the name, terror shot through her system. It was the Curse. Asmos had been there, hiding, waiting, for this exact moment. For her realization of true love. Panic slammed into her chest.

"Emma!" As if from a lifetime away, she heard Damien calling her name. She tried to concentrate, to focus on his voice, to fight off the demon trying to control her, but Asmos was too strong.

"Damien…" If only she could see him, maybe then she could believe that he was still there. That he could still save her. But she was lost in a cloud of darkness, buffered from the outside world by a thick haze of rancid smoke that filled her lungs and choked her.

She reached with her mind, as Damien had taught her to do. She pictured heavy steel walls closing in around her, closing out the darkness. She filled the small room around her with warmth. With love. With a bright, white light.

And suddenly, she could breathe. The overwhelming pressure within her dissipated and her panic receded. She didn't have much time. She had to focus on pushing the demon out. She tried, until tears filled her eyes and ran down her cheeks, but she might as well have been beating her head against the wall.

She turned and sank to the floor, then gasped. She was no longer alone in the stark white room. A woman stood before her draped in a red gossamer gown.

Her heart clenched. "Mummy?" Was it possible that her mother was standing there, clasping her hands in front of her, a sweet, happy smile on her face?

"Hello, Emma."

Pain and longing shot through her. It was her mother's voice—the same tone, the same tilt of her head.

Her mother reached a hand toward her. "Let go,

Emma. Leave all this behind and come with me. There is no more pain where I am. No loneliness. No emptiness. Come be with me."

Fresh tears stained Emma's cheeks. Oh, how she wanted to believe. With all her heart and soul, she wanted to believe that, somehow, her mother was there to take her away from all this, to bring back the joy and happiness of her life before the wolves, before the nightmares.

Emma stood, and her mother took her hands within her own. Emotion filled her, overwhelming her as she felt her mother's gentle touch.

"Emma!" Damien's voice reverberated through her mind, bringing her back, and reminding her where she was, and what was happening. She felt something touch her, but it wasn't her mother. They were no longer touching, and when she looked at her mother, at the perfection in her face, at the love in her eyes, she wished it were true, with all her heart, she wanted it to be true. Please be my mother!

"Focus, Emma," Damien's voice echoed through her mind, bringing with it the realization that her mother wasn't there. It was a ruse to trick her into giving up her soul. Sadness permeated her every fiber as her mother vanished, disappearing along with the bright light and the steel walls.

And she was once again wandering in the dark mist, aware that she wasn't alone as she heard movement in the shadows. Her fear became almost tangible, almost an entity unto itself, as her anxiety grew into a painful knot deep within her.

She had to fight. She had to be strong. She pictured Damien and his steely blue eyes boring into her. Demanding that she focus. Demanding that she concentrate on the stone. She thought of the crystal, remembering the striations and the movements within. She pictured Asmos trapped within the stone the same way she was trapped within the darkness now. But if it was working, she couldn't tell. Nothing changed.

Something in the shadows moved. A dark, unspecified shape that solidified and expanded before her. She froze, staring at it in wide-eyed horror, before something broke loose inside her, and she ran.

"Damien!" she screamed, and then he was standing before her. Relief washed over her like a tidal wave and she rushed to him, throwing her arms around him and clinging to his chest.

He stroked her hair and murmured into her ear. "It's okay. You're okay. I'm here now. Nothing is going to happen to you. I promised you that, didn't I?"

She nodded and, smiling, looked up into his face as tears of joy glittered in her eyes. "Thank you," she whispered. "Thank you for coming for me."

"Focus on my voice, on my touch. I'm here for you." He smiled down at her. And suddenly, his face stretched, and his teeth, long and distorted, burst out of his gums, dripping blood down their sharp points.

Emma screamed and pushed away from him.

"I won't hurt you," he said, garbling something as blood filled his mouth and oozed out the corners.

*Kill him, Emma!*

Damien walked toward her, and suddenly she had a silver dagger in her hand. Horror-struck, she stared at it. He came closer, reaching.

*Kill him!* The voice urged.

"No!" Emma dropped the knife, turned and ran, but fell as the pressure within her grew. She doubled over and grabbed her stomach as pain ripped through her gut. Suddenly the walls were back, surrounding her again. Only she hadn't imagined them. This time they weren't there to comfort, but to imprison.

She placed her hands against them, moving around the perimeter, searching for an opening. Suddenly, they began to move, closing in around her and the only way out, the only escape, was a small dark hole in the floor.

The space between her and the walls tightened, narrowing, pushing her toward the hole. Emma started to cry as panic overwhelmed her, squeezing her chest, stealing her breath.

"It's all right, Emma."

Gulping her tears, Emma turned toward the voice. The walls stopped moving and her mother was back, crouching in front of her, this time dressed in white silk that shimmered in the dim light.

"Stay away from me," Emma sputtered, trying to gasp a breath.

"If you don't let go, you'll be trapped here in the darkness forever. Asmos is in control now. There's nothing you can do."

"Damien," she cried.

"No one can help him now." Her mother's tone was

soft and soothing, but it didn't diminish the fear in Emma's heart. "You're going to kill him," she said. "You won't be able to help yourself, any more than I could help killing Charles."

Emma closed her eyes against the memories assaulting her. "I saw you. I was there."

"I know. I'm sorry for that."

And then the wolves came, one by one they sat by her, the large male laying his head in her lap. She stroked his fur, comforted by his presence, by his warmth. She looked into his brown eyes and saw love, saw compassion. If only she could curl up next to him and go to sleep, then maybe she'd wake up and this nightmare would end.

"We've been waiting a long time for you, Emma. We've missed you. Come with us and you will never have to be scared and alone again."

More than anything Emma wanted to believe her. She wanted to let go. She was so tired of fighting. But she couldn't. She had to hang on just a little longer. For Damien.

Damien lay next to Emma and took a deep breath, feeling the languor of their lovemaking spread through him. He could get used to this, could get used to spending the rest of his life watching over her and taking care of her. He smiled and ran a finger along her jaw.

But she didn't turn to him. "Emma?" And then he smelled it—the brimstone wafting through the room—

and terror gripped his heart. He switched on the bedside lamp next to him and looked down in horror as Emma looked up at him, an evil smile splitting her face.

"Emma!"

Her hand reached for his neck. She grabbed him with her claw-like grip and squeezed, cutting off his airflow. He jerked back, surprised by her strength, by the way her eyes changed, slanting, looking a lot like wolf eyes.

He pulled away from her, backing off the bed, until he heard a low growl from behind him. He stopped and looked over his shoulder. The wolves were surrounding them.

"Lucia!" he yelled, hoping whatever potion the woman had used the last time to scare off the beasts would work once again. Emma lay back on the pillows, staring at him, a wide smile on her face. He eased off the bed, moving slowly and stepped into his pants. He had to get the crystal. He had to draw Asmos out of Emma before she was lost to him forever.

"Lucia!" he yelled again, and was rewarded by the sound of her footsteps running up the stairs. "The wolves are back!" he warned her, then slowly crossed by the snarling beasts to get the duffel bag with the stone.

"Damien, what's the matter?" Emma asked. She chewed on her nail, pouting at him. "Come back to bed."

"I'm coming," he muttered, and grabbed the stone.

"What's that?" she asked.

"A gift." He eased past the wolves who were just sitting there, staring at him. Waiting for Emma to kill him, for the bloodshed to begin.

He climbed back up on the bed and sat across from her.

"Come closer, Damien," she whispered.

"Here, look what I have." He handed her the crystal.

She smiled and took it. "Pretty."

He placed his hands over hers and started to concentrate, to pull the impurities from her system, to shake Asmos loose.

"Is it working?" Emma asked, smiling. She pulled her hands out from under his and ran them up his arms, pulling him closer. "Don't you want to make love to me, Damien?"

He ignored her and focused his energy on the stone, on the evil within her.

Lucia walked into the room and gasped. "What's happening?" she demanded. Her shrill voice rattled, breaking his concentration. Not that he'd made any progress. "You said he was gone!" Lucia continued. "You said we had nothing to worry about."

Her words sliced Damien through and through. Yes, he'd been wrong. He'd screwed up. And he only had one chance to make it right.

"I made a mistake. Now can you help me fix it and get rid of these wolves?"

She held up the rag and lit it. A noxious smoke filled the room. Whatever she was burning turned his stomach. Emma hissed and drew back from him. The wolves started to bark and whine. Lucia moved further into the room, swinging her arm back and forth, driving Emma into a fury. She launched herself at him, biting and scratching, trying to tear him apart.

The wolves jumped into the fray and attacked. He fought them off, but suffered multiple scratches and bites before the room filled with smoke and they ran off down the stairs, disappearing somewhere within the house. The rag lay on the carpet and had set fire to the wool fibers.

Lucia lay on the ground next to it, blood seeping from a gash in her head. He couldn't tell if she was breathing. But worse was Emma, and the red glow in her eyes. He could see nothing left of the woman he loved. She'd become Asmos.

"Emma! Look at me. Focus! Can you hear me?" He grabbed her hands and put them back on the crystal. "Fight him, Emma. Fight!"

She pulled back and stepped off the bed. In desperation Damien grabbed the stone, and alone started the ritual that would pull Asmos out of Emma and into the crystal sphere. He only hoped it wasn't too late. He couldn't lose her. She'd become…everything.

He started the meditation process, whispering the Latin incantations, and tried to focus, tried to distance himself from the fear flooding his system. He breathed deeply, counting backward, feeling the energy expand in his chest as he moved into the zone, going to the place he mentally needed to be to pull Asmos to him.

He put all of himself into it, giving everything he

had, and he still couldn't seem to pull it off. The ancient demon was just too big, too powerful. Damien closed his eyes, and entered a deep trance using all his strength, focusing all his energy, knowing he was making himself vulnerable to Emma and any attack she chose to launch.

As he worked, he felt Asmos coming toward him, felt his bulk, his hate. With all his mental strength, Damien wrestled the demon in a tug-of-war for Emma's soul. And, for a second, Damien could swear he felt Emma's presence, could swear he could hear her calling to him. It wasn't too late!

"Emma!" he yelled. "Help me! Focus, Emma. Fight!"

"You'll never win, Damien. Lick your wounds and leave." The voice, sounding so much like Emma's, filled him. And he knew he would never leave. He would stay until the death, fighting for Emma's soul. No matter what it took, he would not lose her.

"Damien!" He was really there. Emma could feel his presence in the darkness. With her heart and soul, she reached for him, clinging to all she had left—her love for him. She tried to focus as he told her, on his voice, his touch. But she couldn't find him.

She spun around looking, but saw nothing through the gray mist. Worse, her mother and the wolves were gone. She was alone in the dark among the shadows. As she ran through the maze of corridors, she lost her balance. She tripped, falling, suddenly sliding toward the hole. She screamed, as she careened toward the edge, toward the dark abyss, knowing that if she went over, she would never return.

As if pushed by Asmos himself, she couldn't stop, and slid right over the edge. At the last second, she reached out and grabbed hold of the lip. She looked down into the darkness, and saw a light beyond the black horizon. The heady scent of earth, of forest reached her, and a cool mist touched her face.

She was so tired of fighting, of trying to hang on. Her arms ached, and as she tried to pull herself up, tried to adjust her weight, she realized that it was time to face the inevitable. Time to do as her mother asked and just let go.

Tears filled her eyes as she loosened her grip. "I'm sorry, Damien."

Suddenly, she was being pulled back. Yanked out of the hole, out of the dark fog. Nausea turned her stomach, and a cold sheen of sweat covered her skin. But the shadows were receding, the pressure and the overwhelming feelings of fear and hopelessness.

"Damien?" Had he found a way to save her?

A sharp pain pierced her neck. Her head swam, and she felt weak and tired. Then the fear came back, but this time it was different. Asmos was gone, she knew that, and yet, something was wrong. She couldn't open her eyes.

She couldn't feel anything.

And she was so tired. Too tired to fight anymore. Too tired to care what was happening. Sleep overcame her, drowning out her last thought, her last hope.

*Damien.*

# Chapter 20

Damien had no way of judging how long the battle had raged on when at last, exhausted and drenched with sweat, he finally found a weakness, a foothold within. He grabbed hold of Asmos's essence and pulled. Feeling the demon break loose, he dug in with all his power, newfound and old, and pulled Asmos out of Emma and into the crystal sphere.

Exhausted, he crumpled to the ground, breathing deeply, afraid for a moment, to open his eyes. Afraid that somehow Asmos had tricked him again and when he saw Emma he'd know in his heart of hearts that he'd failed and she was lost to him forever. Unable to wait any longer, he opened his eyes. And cried out loud in anguish.

Nicholai was lying over Emma, drinking what was left of Asmos's essence from her blood. Shocked, Damien let loose a tormented roar and launched himself onto his brother.

Nicholai easily averted him, knocked Damien back to the floor and rubbed the back of his hand across his bloody mouth. "You can thank me later, bro. You never would have got that demon out of her alone."

Damien stared at Emma's pale skin and couldn't think, couldn't talk. The all-encompassing pain slicing through him, filled every fiber in his being.

"If you love her, brother, give her life. Save her. Take a sweet taste, then give her your blood. Embrace who you are. What you are."

"No!" Damien protested, and dropped his head into his hands. *How could this have happened?*

"She's dying, brother. Slipping away right now. In another minute, the battle for her soul will be over. But you can give her another chance at life. You can give her the gift of immortality."

Damien stared up at him through blurred eyes filled with hate. "And make her a monster?"

"Is that what you are?" Nicholai mocked. "I thought you only saw me that way."

Pain seared through Damien's soul; it was like nothing he'd ever felt before. "How could you do this? To me?"

"Why not? Because we're brothers? Because we have some paternal bond that bridges us beyond the veil of what we are?" He cocked a smile. "Well, you're right. That's why I did it. I saved her for you. Another minute and she would have been lost, floundering in some demon dimension, or sucked into the bowels of hell. No one knows for sure. All we do know is that Asmos had her, and he wasn't going to give her back."

Damien stood and picked up Emma's satin night-gown, and crunched it into a tight ball. "My fault," he muttered.

Nicholai grinned. "Of course it's your fault. You fell in love and couldn't keep your pants zipped."

"Get away from her," Damien demanded, and pulled the sheets up over Emma's body.

Nicholai opened his arms in a wide gesture. "Hey, I tried to warn you. I tried to stop all this from happening, but the little spitfire was stronger than I expected."

Damien's rage bubbled to the boiling point. He knew his brother had always been able to spin any situation to his advantage, but this took the cake. "You expect me to believe you were here to help? That what you did, *everything you did,* you did for us?"

"You can believe whatever you want, dear brother. But if you ever want to see blondie here open those blue peepers again, you'd better get to work. The clock is a-ticking."

Damien looked back at Emma, who was growing paler by the moment. As horrific as it sounded, he knew his brother was right. If he was going to save Emma, he had to do what he swore to the Cadre, what he'd sworn to himself, he would never do. He had to exchange blood with Emma in order to give her the "gift" of life.

He dropped the crystal with Asmos trapped within onto the floor, then climbed up on the bed next to Emma. He pulled her limp body into his arms and held her close. Her pulse weakened, growing fainter by the minute. He couldn't lose her. He would do *anything* to save her. And, like it or not, this was the *only* thing that *could* save her.

"I'm sorry," he whispered, then, closing his eyes, brushed his lips against the delicate skin of Emma's neck, and bit down, taking a sweet taste. Warm blood trickled into his mouth, filling him with her essence, with her sweetness, and he could feel her love for him, could feel the goodness in her soul, and it made him want to weep.

Then he pulled back and bit his wrist until the blood flowed freely, then pressed the open vein to her lips. "Choose me, Emma. Choose life," he begged, and hoped it wasn't too late.

Something wet and sweet dripped across Emma's parched lips. She was so thirsty, she was just sick with it. Her stomach rumbled and turned as the liquid sluiced down her throat. Her headache and lightheadedness were dissipating, and she was beginning to feel a tad stronger.

Suddenly she was just starved, and nothing could fulfill her but the sweetness flowing into her mouth. She reached up, pulling the source closer and drank greedily, feeling herself change once again, but this time the darkness and fear within her were gone and all she felt was love and the absolute joy of being loved in return.

Soon, she was strong enough to be aware of her surroundings. She was still lying on Damien's bed. She cracked open her eyes, almost expecting to see him lying beside her, sleeping. As if everything that had happened had just been a terrible dream.

But he wasn't lying there, and he wasn't sleeping. He was looking at her with a haunted look of regret filling his eyes.

"What is it?" she asked, at once afraid for him. "Is everything all right?"

He smiled, but it was a look sad enough to break her heart. "How much do you remember?"

"About what? Damien, you're scaring me." She sat up, and then noticed the shambles of the room, noticed Lucia lying on the floor. "Oh, my God." She jumped out of the bed and ran to her. "Lucia!" Lucia stirred slightly, as Emma pulled on her shoulder. "She has a nasty gash on her head. What happened in here?"

"Get dressed. I'll carry her downstairs," Damien said as he bent beside Lucia and felt for her pulse. "It's strong." He picked her up and carried her down the stairs. Emma donned her robe and hurried after them. Once she had Lucia settled, she pulled Damien into the kitchen. "Tell me what happened to her."

"We had a scuffle with the wolves. We—" his voice broke, and he turned away. "We almost lost you."

Dread dropped a sickening thud to the bottom of her stomach, and Emma knew she hadn't been dreaming. "Asmos?" she whispered. "The Curse?"

He nodded.

She turned toward the sink, and grasped the tile. "I remember I was on the edge of a hole. I don't know where it came from, or where it went, but I almost fell in." She turned and looked at him. "I would have fallen, but at the last minute, I was yanked out of the darkness. You saved me. You brought me back."

He shook his head and turned away.

She grabbed his shoulder and forced him around. "You saved me."

"Not me," he whispered.

She stared into his eyes, as confusion filled her and what she saw there made her afraid to ask. But she had to know. "Then who?"

"Nicholai."

A shudder moved through her.

"By sucking Asmos's essence out of your blood, Nicholai weakened him to the point that I was able to pull him out of you and into the stone."

Emma looked around her. "Then where did Nicholai go?"

"Gone. With the stone."

Her eyes widened. "He left with the demon? What will the Cadre say?"

"It doesn't matter. Nothing matters anymore. I'm so sorry, Emma. It's my fault. I couldn't live without you. It was selfish, I know, to turn you, to force you into this world, into the dark. I just couldn't let you die."

Her eyes widened. "What are you talking about?" But as she stared at him, at the guilt and anguish on his face, the realization of what he was talking about struck her.

She'd thought it was because she was tired, because of the nightmare she'd lived through, that everything seemed different. Her vision was deeper, sharper, colors more monochromatic. Smells were stronger, and almost offensive. And she was so hungry—a yearning hunger unlike she'd ever felt.

She brought her fingers to her neck, feeling the ache, the jagged edges of the wound. Panic sliced through her. "You fed off me?" she asked unbelieving.

"I brought you back. I gave you the gift."

She turned away from him, trying to comprehend what he was saying. "Am I dead?"

"You are no longer human."

She moved to the kitchen table and collapsed into a chair. She'd died tonight. She hadn't fallen down the hole, fallen into the darkness, but she'd still died.

And Damien had brought her back. Only he'd brought her back different.

"You said Nicholai sucked out Asmos's essence." She swallowed. "From me."

Damien nodded.

"And if you hadn't done what you did…" She groped, trying to understand.

He pulled out a chair and sat across from her. "Then

you wouldn't be here talking to me now." He stared at her, then ran a finger down her cheek. "Your scars are gone."

"So is my humanity." A hunger cramp ripped through her stomach. She bent over, clutching her stomach as her teeth pushed through her gums. Horrified, she reached up and touched the sharp points.

"You need to feed," he said. "And soon. Then you'll feel better."

"Feed? On what?" she asked horrified. "I will not hurt any animals," she said, vehemently, thinking of Angel, still sleeping peacefully upstairs in her room, she hoped.

"You don't have to. You're not a monster," he said, more to himself than to her.

Her heart softened, as she heard the anguish in his tone. "No, I'm like you. And, like you, I choose not to kill. Like you, I will work to make life better for myself, and for those I love."

He pulled her into his arms, and held her close. "I wish I could see me the way you see me."

"Do you believe I'm evil?" she asked.

"No," he choked, and drew back to look her in the eyes. "Never."

"But I've been touched by evil. Just like before, when I was human. It was my choice whether or not to embrace it."

"But you're not human. Not anymore. It will take a while to adjust, to forgive."

"That might be true, but I still have a choice. And I choose you, Damien. You kept me from falling into the abyss. You saved me. You brought me back. And with your blood, you've given me a new life to live and explore. I choose you, Damien. I choose love."

\* \* \* \* \*

*For a sneak preview of Marie Ferrarella's*
*DOCTOR IN THE HOUSE,*
*coming to NEXT in September,*
*please turn the page.*

**He** didn't look like an unholy terror.

But maybe that reputation was exaggerated, Bailey DelMonico thought as she turned in her chair to look toward the doorway.

The man didn't seem scary at all.

Dr. Munro, or Ivan the Terrible, was tall, with an athletic build and wide shoulders. The cheekbones beneath what she estimated to be day-old stubble were prominent. His hair was light brown and just this side of unruly. Munro's hair looked as if he used his fingers for a comb and didn't care who knew it.

The eyes were brown, almost black as they were

aimed at her. There was no other word for it. Aimed. As if he was debating whether or not to fire at point-blank range.

Somewhere in the back of her mind, a line from a B movie, "Be afraid—be very afraid…" whispered along the perimeter of her brain. Warning her. Almost against her will, it caused her to brace her shoulders. Bailey had to remind herself to breathe in and out like a normal person.

The chief of staff, Dr. Bennett, had tried his level best to put her at ease and had almost succeeded. But an air of tension had entered with Munro. She wondered if Dr. Bennett was bracing himself as well, bracing for some kind of disaster or explosion.

"Ah, here he is now," Harold Bennett announced needlessly. The smile on his lips was slightly forced, and the look in his gray, kindly eyes held a warning as he looked at his chief neurosurgeon. "We were just talking about you, Dr. Munro."

"Can't imagine why," Ivan replied dryly.

Harold cleared his throat, as if that would cover the less than friendly tone of voice Ivan had just displayed. "Dr. Munro, this is the young woman I was telling you about yesterday."

Now his eyes dissected her. Bailey felt as if she was undergoing a scalpel-less autopsy right then and there. "Ah yes, the Stanford Special."

He made her sound like something that was listed at the top of a third-rate diner menu. There was enough contempt in his voice to offend an entire delegation from the UN.

Summoning the bravado that her parents always claimed had been infused in her since the moment she first drew breath, Bailey put out her hand. "Hello. I'm Dr. Bailey DelMonico."

Ivan made no effort to take the hand offered to him. Instead, he slid his long, lanky form bonelessly into the chair beside her. He proceeded to move the chair ever so slightly so that there was even more space between them. Ivan faced the chief of staff, but the words he spoke were addressed to her.

"You're a doctor, DelMonico, when I say you're a doctor," he informed her coldly, sparing her only one frosty glance to punctuate the end of his statement.

Harold stifled a sigh. "Dr. Munro is going to take over your education. Dr. Munro—" he fixed Ivan with a steely gaze that had been known to send lesser doctors running for their antacids, but, as always, seemed to have no effect on the chief neurosurgeon "—I want you to award her every consideration. From now on, Dr. DelMonico is to be your shadow, your sponge and your assistant." He emphasized the last word as his eyes locked with Ivan's. "Do I make myself clear?"

For his part, Ivan seemed completely unfazed. He merely nodded, his eyes and expression unreadable. "Perfectly."

His hand was on the doorknob. Bailey sprang to her

feet. Her chair made a scraping noise as she moved it back and then quickly joined the neurosurgeon before he could leave the office.

Closing the door behind him, Ivan leaned over and whispered into her ear, "Just so you know, I'm going to be your worst nightmare."

Bailey DelMonico has finally
gotten her life on track, and is
passionate about her recent career
change. Nothing will stand in the way
of her becoming a doctor...that is,
until she's paired with the sharp-tongued
Dr. Ivan Munro.

Watch the sparks fly in

# Doctor in the House

by *USA TODAY* Bestselling Author

# Marie Ferrarella

Available September 2007

Intrigued? Read more at
**TheNextNovel.com**

HARLEQUIN®
Next™

HN88141

## Romantic
# SUSPENSE

*Sparked by Danger,*
*Fueled by Passion.*

When evidence is found that Mallory Dawes
intends to sell the personal financial information
of government employees to "the Russian,"
OMEGA engages undercover agent Cutter Smith.
Tailing her all the way to France, Cutter is
fighting a growing attraction to Mallory while at
the same time having to determine her connection
to "the Russian." Is Mallory really the mouse in
this game of cat and mouse?

### Look for

# *Stranded with a Spy*

### by *USA TODAY* bestselling author

# Merline Lovelace

### *October 2007.*

# REQUEST YOUR FREE BOOKS!

## 2 FREE NOVELS PLUS 2 FREE GIFTS!

Silhouette®

# n o c t u r n e ™

**Dramatic and Sensual Tales of Paranormal Romance.**

# ATHENA FORCE

*Heart-pounding romance and thrilling adventure.*

## A deadly masquerade

As an undercover asset for the FBI, mafia princess
Sasha Bracciali can deceive and improvise at a
moment's notice. But when she's cut off from
everything she knows, including her FBI-agent
lover, Sasha realizes her deceptions have masked
a painful truth: she doesn't know whom to trust.
If she doesn't figure it out quickly, her most
ambitious charade will also be her last.

### Look for

# CHARADE
by *Kate Donovan*

*Available in October
wherever you buy books.*

# nocturne™

*Look for*

## NIGHT MISCHIEF

*by*

# NINA BRUHNS

Lady Dawn Maybank's worst nightmare
is realized when she accidentally conjures
a demon of vengeance, Galen McManus. What
she doesn't realize is that Galen plans to teach
her a lesson in love—one she'll never forget....

# DARK
## ENCHANTMENTS
▲

*Available October wherever you buy books.*

*Don't miss the last installment of Dark Enchantments,*
*SAVING DESTINY by Pat White, available November.*

**www.eHarlequin.com**          SN61772

# nocturne™

## COMING NEXT MONTH

**#25 NIGHT MISCHIEF • Nina Bruhns**

*Dark Enchantments (Book 3 of 4)*

A thoughtlessly spoken spell conjures Lady Dawn Maybank's worst nightmare—a demon of vengeance. But can Galen McManus teach Dawn the true meaning of love with a lesson she'll never forget?

**#26 DARK LIES • Vivi Anna**

*The Valorian Chronicles*

The last place lycan investigator Jace Jericho wants to go to is San Antonio, surrounded by humans. But his partnership with police escort Tala Channing holds a secret that could renew the boundaries between human relations—or tear them apart....